BEFORE THE
BIG BANG

T0078204

CHAPTER ONE

A person decides to write a fiction when he is free of oppressive rules if he is in a Government job or when he is brought to the writing mode by cupidity. In the case of Ratnakar, who retired recently from a government high school and got more money than he could care to spend, it was not the cupidity, it was the heat that accumulated in him during his tenure as a teacher that prodded him to write a novel that could startle some into believing that he was something more than they found him to be in the world he just left. But the reality is that his colleagues who retired with him or who were still in the school had forgotten about him.

Ratnakar thought about the past and imagined a torn diary.

Thinking of his many class friends, playmates, cinema crazy partners, when he was in class VIII way back in 1950s gave him a frisson of pleasure which was quite unlike anything he could say about his co-workers in the school. He remembered this period chiefly because it was when he was introduced to some persons who were understood to be belonging to a revolutionary party which was, he was told, banned then.

Ratnakar and his friends Jagadish Rao, Diwakar Singh, D Subba Rao, who came greatly under the influence of a teacher of the school they were reading in, followed

1

his instructions, philosophy and way of life to a T. It was P Chalpati, their teacher, who introduced them to these persons symbolizing for them the mystique of revolution and strength. This single event changed their world outlook, if such a thing then existed for them, for ever. Even before they deserted shorts—half pants—they felt far ahead of the times intellectually because they asked them basic but searching questions. Time alone could tell whether their assessment, such as it was, was correct about themselves.

Throwing his initial hesitation, Ratnakar put the question: "If it's accepted Congress fought for Independence and got it for the country, then why shouldn't we support it?"

"Congress is a political party. Communist Part of India is a political party. Then why should we support one and not the other? What is the difference?" Jagadish asked.

"Jinna took away Pakistan." Subba Rao raising his head slowly, said, "Why shouldn't we support a Hindu party? Why Communist Party of India?"

Of course these boys were not satisfied with the answers they received from them. And yet . . .

Officially speaking, there was no office then of the CPI in Kadampur, a railway town he was talking about evidently because it was not permitted to work openly. It was though functioning secretly from underground and its location appeared to these boys mysteriously attractive. One Mr. Jackson, a supporter of the Party, who lived in a house near a walled railway ground and beside a big drain, allowed his small dwelling to be used by the Party for purposes of meetings and writing posters at times. The wall was broken at a point, and a couple of cemented slabs laid on the huge drain which made the approach to his house from the playground easier. There was of course a normal path to his house but this meant passing by a cluster of houses at Netaji Pally.

Ratnakar couldn't see anybody writing posters during his three or visits to this place along with his friends though posters written on old newspapers were found scattered all over the room. They were asked to bring in the old newspapers with them whenever they visited the spot which they did. To say this place had an aura of mystery about it to them would be stating the obvious and though they were attracted hugely to the idea of society's change, they felt frustrated after some visits. They were lads of 14 to 16 years and were genuinely afraid of sailing in uncharted waters of politics or whatever it was.

These boys actually lived in two worlds, one of the schools, the other of a developing idea and ideology the contours of which were still not very clear. They attended classes, worked out exercises, played games, read magazines and novels. They also went to private tutors, and prepared for the exams like others. But something did happen to their psyche which was making them different from others, and goading them to take an alternative path.

What they failed to get in their secret trips to Mr. Jackson's office was surprisingly provided by the announcement of General Election in the form of an opportunity to do something openly which was to their like. But here again they were stumped because a couple of communist leaders who could be candidates for the state assembly legislature seats were still behind bars. In the tutorial run by P Chalpati, where Ratnakar,Jagadish and Diwakar were enrolled there was an additional teacher who taught maths as efficiently as Chalpati did English grammar. Clearly this combination drew good students.

When the teaching was over, Mr. P Chalpati asked them," Do you know something new is going to happen in this town soon?"

"What?" Ratnakar couldn't guess anything.

"Why put a new burden on them?" The maths teacher said to Chalpati."Leave them alone."

"Election . . . you mean . . ." Jagadish ventured to reply.

"Yes. You rightly guessed." Chalpati said," If you feel a change is necessary in the present setup or your environment you can participate in it. It's new for all of us. If you want some experience of what election is about here's a chance for you to get into the storm. I can arrange for it. In fact I'd like you to get into this action"

Since Chalpati was much more knowledgeable about politics than any other teacher they came across, just as he was about English grammar, they were fascinated, influenced and encouraged by his words. There was no question but to follow his advice. He just had to describe it to them in his inimitable phraseology.

In the meanwhile in Jackson's house surfaced a face of the real Party in the figure of Prafulla Maity who asked them to write posters in Hindi, with the slogans and themes concerning people's demands provided by him. Comrade Prafulla Maity gave them to understand that the Communist Party of India was in no position to contest the Kadampur assembly seat as the leaders Hari Narayan Mishra and some others were still in jail, and also because there was no grassroots level work done among workers or common people, a necessary condition before a candidate was nominated. In fact the CPI was quite an unknown entity then in the emerging political scenario at Kadampur. Indeed,except for Prafulla Maity no other face was open to the public gaze. The communists, they were told, were working from underground. They were feared and loved alike by the people.

Though the picture changed after the announcement of the General Election, the CPI could not take advantage of the easing of the situation for it: it couldn't put up a candidate for the assembly seat.

Chalpati called some of them to his house one day. He began in his usual way, "I want you to work for a candidate in this election. He is educated and a perfect gentleman. What's more he understands the problems of workers and sympathetic to them. I'd a talk with him. He's short of workers—workers for election purposes."

"But what about CPI and Com. Maity. Haven't we committed in a manner to him?" Ratnakar paused thinking he'd said too much.

"I think we should go to Prafulla 'da first to understand clearly his position in relation to this election." Diwakar said.

"But who's the candidate you've referred to?"Subbarao asked. "Turning to his friends, he added," When Prafulla da has no candidate then it's immaterial to him whom we support."

Just then they heard the sound of a cycle being stood on its stand near the door. It was Com. Prafulla Maity. who first greeted Mr. Chalpati who answered saying," Come in Mr. Maity. Please sit here." They were sitting on the mat, silent.

"Chalpatibabu, you're right about Mr.Nair—Mr HK Nair. The district committee decided in favour of supporting Mr. Nair. If he's nominated by Krishak Mazdoor Praja Party, we shall have no objection. We shall canvass for him as against Congress and others."Com. Maity announced.

'In a day or two the KMPP's office will be sending the official papers to Mr. Nair nominating him as their candidate. You may rest assured about it."Chalpati said.

"You should work for H K Nair."Turning to Ratnakar and others, Com Maity said, "You know A.Mehata is a socialist. So we're supporting his KMPP."

"That's what we were discussing before you came here. I'll find out from Mr. Nair what kind of work he needs from them. They are too young to do much but can handle mike for announcement purposes." Chalpati said.

"Some of them write good posters." Com Maity added, laughing.

"Do they, really?" Chalpati was astonished. Maity just nodded in agreement.

Kadampur was bustling with political activities with Congress, Jana Sangh, HM, KMPP and other independent candidates setting in motion their propaganda machinery asking people to give their votes to their respective candidates and parties. Since this was the first ever election after the promulgation of the Constitution, the people here were still to understand the implications of vote and its relation to their aspirations. The people were certainly curious but not enthusiastic about it. The town consisted largely of railway workers and employees living in quarters in railway area. And the railway being a Government of India concern and the Centre being ruled by the Congress, the employees' mind could be presumed to be set already in favour of the Congress as voting against it meant being disloyal to the employers. When none else than Pt. Nehru,adding an element of surprise,came to this town and held a meeting to ask the people to vote for the Congress candidates in the area the doubt, if any, as to who would be the winner was wiped out. The balance tilted heavily in favor of the Congress candidate Maulana Mohammad Ali, who simply sat smug and did not stir much thereafter.

Ratnakar and his friends Subbarao and Diwakar did make two or three rounds of the town in the amplifier and mike-fitted rickshaw urging people to vote for their Krishak Mazdoor Praja Party candidate H K Nair and had the novel experience of being cornered at a couple of places in south side.

"Why did you enter this area? This is railway officers' area. No mike here. Get the hell out of this place."Someone shouted from behind their rickshaw.

"But we're canvassing for our candidate. This is election time." Ratnakar tried to argue with the group of six including two elderly men who surrounded the rickshaw.

"No canvassing here. We shall snatch and seize your amplifier and mike." One muscular looking man said.

"Let them go. They're just boys—innocent boys." An elderly man intervened.

"No sound. Remember."

Ratnakar and his friend sitting in the rickshaw heard this. The rickshaw driver did not need any further instruction from them to move

They were deeply disappointed when Congress won defeating Mr. Nair and others. One independent candidate, Sher Singh Kochar, who spent more money than the total amount of all others, on propaganda, lost his deposit. The boys took the defeat of their candidate as humiliation and jointly decided to never do this kind of work ever. It was study and study and nothing else for them from now onward.

Industrious students as they were, all of them passed their respective exams and were promoted to the next higher classes. But Ratnakar decided to leave this school because he felt the standard of teaching had come down much in it and because some well-wishers assured him that he'd a good chance to be admitted in the railway boys' school which was reputed to have very high quality of teaching as the staff were eminently educated and motivated Non-railway boys could be admitted in a class if two or three seats remained empty after admission of railway employees' wards, and after a test and on basis of their previous school record. It was not so much the test or the mark sheet of the last school but the kind-heartedness and generosity of the teachers in the railway boys' school that smoothed his admission in it. But was it just a change from one school to another or something more ?

The whole academic and social milieu changed. Except for some, most of the students appeared well-dressed, well-fed and well-informed. His class-mates enjoyed the additional facilities of books from the library which could put to shame any other library of any other school. Though Ratnakar tried to meet his old friends he left in the previous school such meetings gradually decreased in frequency. The going in this school could have proved difficult for him and he would have found himself unfit in this milieu had it not been for a change in economic and social status that occurred in his family just prior to his admission: the change was brought about by his father's shifting of his shop from a less profitable area to a bigger place on the ever-crowded main road. The business flourished. So money was not a problem for him for private tuition and spending among friends.

Just a little before Ratnakar joined railway high school his family's economic condition was not in a good shape with troubles brewing at many points, some of them seemingly insurmountable at times. It was a tale of instinct for survival. But he had his moments of happiness in his family of eight members and a large number of friends and playmates. It was not the events so much as the idealism that enlivened the course of his journey from childhood onwards. Actually his father always prodded him to read the Ramayana to him whenever he was at leisure and encouraged him to be a wrestler.

"Abey Ratna, I heard you joined Sher Singh's akhara. Is it true?" There was more surprise than sarcasm in Laxman's voice, one of his playmates.

"Yes I did. So what?" Ratnakar replied somewhat angrily.

"But you're so thin and skinny you can't raise even the smallest mallet there. You're really a wonder. "It was sarcasm indeed from Laxman.

"Right now the ustad is teaching me only wrestling. I'll cross the bridge when mace raising exercise comes. It'll take drinking of milk in plenty. That's all." He tried to put a stop to the inquisition.

"But we know you don't like milk. You can't stand even its smell. How'll you drink milk and that too in plenty?" Even Nanha remarked.

There was no way but to take it all but he continued to go to the Ustad's akhara, the wrestling place. because he found there a couple of boys of his age group with some similarities in body build. He knew he couldn't be easily outwitted by any one of them in the tricks department of wrestling which he had already mastered.

The very appearance of Nanaku, a barber by profession, who used to visit their shop on call or even without it, sent a shiver of chill down their spine. His small box containing hair-cutting machine, long thin blade, comb and scissors symbolized a mercilessness perpetrated on his head full of long hair which he fancied much. One thing he didn't like in his father then was his forcing him to have a wrestler's haircut which meant only the thinnest of hair on the scalp. If there was any point of revolt against his father it was this occasion. But after joining the akhara, the resistance to the haircut melted.

Though Kadampur was not a village but a big railway town it was no stranger to Ramleela which became an annual event in their locality. It was organized during winter traditionally. There was a big sprawling vacant spot facing their shop on the other side of the road, at a little distance. Ratnakar couldn't avoid going to it even if he wanted to, in his childhood, because it was so near and also because he liked Hanuman's character in it Though he had yet to memorize Hanuman Chalisa in full, he surely had read it over forty times because, he was told, this could really subdue and expel the evil forces and wipe out dangers and destroy enemies. In the Ramleela ground though there was some arrangement of mat for the audience, they generally carried small mats or canvas bags to sit on. As soon as the light was arranged on the stage with more than half a dozen petromaxes, the jostling and scuffle used to start for the front and advantageous space. He was caught in one of such melees, and what was worse, somebody stabbed a person from behind and his cries of help amid commotion led to a stampede of fleeing persons. Ratnakar ran faster than ever towards his house leaving the sack there.

As soon as the door was opened, and he got in, he said to his father,"Close it and lock it also. There was a brawl in the Ramleela. Some ruffian has stabbed a man."

As no other member of his family was interested in seeing the Ramleela,they were preparing to sleep when he thumped the door. His father didn't need his instruction to close and lock the door from inside as the noise of people shouting and running helter-skelter rose to a peak by then.

"How did it happen? Do you know who was knifed?" His father asked him.

"It all started with a struggle for the front space. But it happened daily. I don't know who was stabbed. But I can guess who knifed him was. It must be that drunkard Jhagru." Ratnakar said, collecting his wits, after the disturbing event.

"Now you won't go to Ramleela tomorrow even if it's staged tomorrow." His mother intervened. "Your Ramleela must end here. Have you understood what I said?"

Ramleela continued to be organized during winter annually as usual at the same spot even after this incident, but Ratnakar stopped going to it after his traumatic experience. He kept his final date with that.

Banwarilal Dikshit was his akhara-partner, classmate and ubiquitous friend. In the front spacious room of his house there was a big raised space for the cushion where four persons could be comfortably accommodated to play any kind of playing-card games with enough room left for Dikshit's mother who was an invariable non-participant partner in the games. But she enjoyed giving running commentary on the game and why one was surely going to lose it. As Dikshit's house opened on the main road and remained open most of the time one could always find him along with another companion just talking when not playing anything and could join them.

It was summer. The school was closed for recess for two months as usual. Because of similarity of Dikshit's interests with his own, he used to come here, a little after breakfast, and stayed there till meal time. Dikshit's father was a non-interfering type of person. So the fun continued uninterrupted with his mother participating in whatever was played or talked about considering all of them as her children evident in her domineering matronliness but with a partiality for Dikshit because he was her only child.

But he was shocked because the Ustad selected Ratnakar for junior wrestling competition on Ramnavami Day at Dhan Singh ground from his akhara, the wrestling place, which was situated in his plot. This led to the beginning of a rift at many levels about which the ustad was not aware.

But Ratnakar was not prepared for this kind of demonstration. It was not easy, playing wrestler. Should he walk out of the dangal, the competition or not? put him in a dilemma. The turning point for him had come.

CHAPTER TWO

That Ratnakar's selection for Junior Wrestling Competition was mired in misunderstanding if not mischief became clear when the ustad (Guru) clarified it was not Ratnakar but Banwarilal who was actually selected by him. Like so many misunderstandings whose originators remained untraced to the last, the progenitor of this misunderstanding remained unknown. For Ratnakar it was a relief: for Banwarilal this clarification was a natural justice.

The day after the wrestling tournament in which neither Dikshit nor Ratnakar participated, the sun rose in the east and everything concerning gathering at Dikshit's place fell into its regular pattern. But Ratnakar's contact with this place became less frequent as some old friends pressed him to renew relations with them at cigarette—wali auntie's house where they congregated to play one thing or another. Her house was situated down the main road in an interior lane with ample open space. Her husband after breakfast used to leave the house with bags full of cigarette cartons on both sides of the cycle and stacks on the carrier to sell them and as she had no child of her own, she had the whole house to herself. The auntie allowed the boys to play in there more to relieve her boredom and loneliness than for anything else. She was fairly wheatish and her betel-chewing habit gave a red glow to her lips. She liked the companionship of these boys immensely which she did not hide as she seldom expressed annoyance at their pranks or even when any domestic utensil fell or broke because of them.

Like other boys, Ratnakar was passing through a change in his person and the atmosphere around him, and each experience was taking a toll of his stable temperament. It was as if Time had begun to unfold its mystery in one encounter after another. When he should be sharing his thoughts with others he found himself closing in and being reticent because he thought his reasoning might not be correct and acceptable. If he became introvert, his loss of confidence somewhere was responsible for it.

One of the auntie's or her husband's relatives surfaced in her house from nowhere and though not a regular visitor he came often. He wasn't young but not old and looked distinguished and somewhat striking with collyrium-eyes. This man had a way of joking which set the auntie laughing. One of the boys confided to Ratnakar,"Our auntie behaves towards us differently when that new fair man is around. If she doesn't want us here or doesn't like us I won't come here." He obviously did not like the collyrium-eyed man's presence here. The boy came very close in relation to her but felt frustrated because he did not own her affection. Nobody had a proprietary right to this emotion. Either it was there or it wasn't. Of course it was his erroneous thinking. The reality might be quite different. Could human relation be ruptured in this way? What the auntie thought about him was not taken into consideration by the frustrated boy.

Auntie's place was like a cool lake with birds playing in its still waters and fluttering above them when they fancied it. The intrusion of this stranger who was not like them disturbed the peace and the balance of the lake. One by one the birds began to disperse leaving it perhaps alone.

Ratnakar, after a couple of visits to the auntie's place at his friends' persuasion, dropped going there because he had more pressing things to do : The economic reality had forced him to help his father in the shop.

Ratnakar was too weak or worked too hard in the shop in that summer that he became ill. After two days it was confirmed it was, in the local parlance, small pox. That year many contracted this disease, particularly children. As there was no medicine for it once one became its victim, he was confined to bed at home with restrictions imposed. A small room was rented in the back of his house exclusively for him. With bubbles erupting all over his body he was in constant pain But cleanliness was arranged by his parents by changing linen after two days if not every day, with small branches of neem leaves set on a nearby chair.

He felt pain and loneliness of a kind he never felt before. Though he got immediate response whenever he called somebody; he knew he was all alone in the world he was pushed into. One day one of his friends, Shivbachan, brought him two novels, hesitating and doubting whether he would read them in that state. He wasn't sure if he was doing the right thing. But he couldn't think of a better way of showing his friendly feelings for him. By chance he came to enquire about him the next day also when Ratnaakar, pointing to the books he gave yesterday,now lying on the table,said," You may take them back. Did you buy these books for me, or were they in your possession already?"

"What's that to you? You should read them. Read them at your liberty."

"But I'd already read them."

"What?" Shivbachan was astounded. "You read the two novels in one day. Normally, they should have taken at least ten days to finish. If you weren't ill I'd have rated it a third rate joke."

"I'm not joking, brother. In fact I'm asking you to bring two more novels if it's not a bother to you."

"Well, I'm a member of a library at Bhawanipur, too. These books were certainly mine. I'll bring a couple of fictions from there also, but it may take a day or two. Don't worry. In the meanwhile I'll be sending you through somebody some detective fictions. "As Shivbachan had dropped in on way to school, he was in a hurry to run for it.

Ratnakar smiled when he heard these assuring words. When he went away Ratnakar came back to himself and to his suffering and boredom. It was during this period that he developed a hunger for books especially fictions. If he read Sharad Chandra, he read Bhagwati Charan Varma, Jai Shankar Prasad and Jainendra K also. Magazines were added to his diet when he had recovered but still convalescing. It didn't need any philosopher to tell him about the necessity of studying books to find solace in life. Small pox which had left ugly scars on his body and face, and which took almost six months to smooth somewhat, made him a different person book wise. If God existed, he wondered,why He created diseases. Perhaps he might never get back the answer; the question troubled him often nevertheless.

CHAPTER THREE

The last few days of his isolation, before he was declared fit to move in the open and rejoin school (mercifully his sickness fell in the period of school's two-month summer holidays) were full of strange images and feelings He didn't think much or recapitulated little when reading fictions. But when a novel was finished, its characters would crowd before his eyes Their presence would be so overwhelming that he would hear their steps, soft and distinct. The days passed off quietly in this manner but nights were full of storms. After night's meal, he'd himself bolt the room's door from inside and start reading in the lantern's light till he felt sleepy. Within hours of getting into the sleep's dark cover, he'd hear sounds of stone being thrown on the tin roof or the devils dancing on it . . . Heavily perspiring, he'd open his eyes to only find everything quiet. Then he'd change the side and go to sleep immediately.

"Who's this person inside the room?" This was a girl's voice. Not from dream world of night, but day's real world.

"We're new-comers here, Sipra. Let's familiarize ourselves first with the neighborhood." A mature woman replied to the girl. Clearly, Ratnakar could understand the adjoining house was rented out, and the new folk had already occupied it.

"I'm curious about the people's going in and coming out of this room with food and the left-over and cutlery" The girl was speaking." May I have a peep into the room, Ma?"The open room was just four steps away from where they were talking.

"No." Her mother shouted in a sudden burst of anger." You won't . . ."

Just then Ratnakar's mother came out with a glass and a green coconut's emptied shell. The girl's mother advanced a step towards her, and said," We couldn't talk with each other though we became your neighbour two days ago. We're a bit curious about who lives in the room you're coming from. So . . ."

"Oh! He's my son. "Ratnakar's mother answered." He was under the spell of small pox. He recovered and is all right now, from day before yesterday he'd started taking bath. We shall go to worship Goddess Shitala today."

"So he's regained health."

"Yes. He's all right except for some marks on his face which I hope will disappear in a month's time."

"Thank God."

Ratnakar heard part of this conversation and was mildly surprised to learn that a girl wanted to have a peep into the room.

Holidays over, the schools reopened. Ratnakar had eaten enough fruits to last one whole year. As a result, he looked far from emaciated when he joined the school. Indeed, he was bubbling with energy. The next door girl, Sipra's initial enthusiasm about him having subsided, he concentrated on studies of text books, and other school activities. She was a class higher than he was and claimed to be better at mathematics in the class than anybody else. And he was no good at mathematics. So there was not much common ground between them, academically speaking.

Sipra's father was a railway employee. With him stayed his younger brother who was yet to be employed. This was a foursome family, keeping to themselves. There was a big neem tree between their houses which narrowed the passage to a set of common latrines for tenants. This passage also led to a door which opened to a vast stretch of ground full of wild plants. Some people used a portion, clearly demarcated and fenced-off, of this extensive place, as a spot of relieving themselves in early mornings and evenings.

One morning, when Ratnakar was enjoying his breakfast, he remembered a part of the dream he had the previous night. It was actually an intrusion. Years earlier he used to roam the back field, with an old cycle rim, driving it with a small stick placing it in its back slope. The field had many ups and downs, appearing mounds to him, and when the wheel would seem to be detaching from the stick he'd make the sound of accelerator from mouth, putting more speed in his run. But the images of the previous night were far from enjoyable.

When he was driving the wheel in this manner, he suddenly became aware that somebody was following him with speed, pursuing him madly, chasing him for a mysterious purpose. Whichever turn he took, the chaser did the same. Ratnakar collected enough courage to stand and look back. The pursuer was undoubtedly racing towards him, with a wooden sandal in his raised hand. It flashed into his mind instantly that it was Bhasmasur, the demon, and none else, who was gifted with the strange-powered sandal that could turn into ashes anybody, man, demon, even god only if he succeeded in putting it on anybody's head. Off went the cycle rim and the stick. He fled from the demon who was coming closer to him to put the dreaded wooden sandal on his head. If he wanted to save himself, he must race and race yet faster.

Breathing hard, he was nearing a place which appeared familiar to him. He knew this was the backside of Lily's house. Lily and he played together in this house just some years ago. Didn't they share the same jokes and play with the dheki (the pounding machine) with the smell of paddy all around. Surely she'd save him from Bhasmasur. She was a brave girl, that little fair goddess. She could outwit the demon. She was his buddy, yes she was.

He didn't remember whether he entered that house. Perhaps the dream just ended there. He couldn't be sure if it was a happy dream or an ominous one. Ratnakar concentrated on finishing the breakfast because he had to do some homework before he went to school.

CHAPTER FOUR

Seeing a group of friends in front of Banwarilal's house, Ratnakar braked his cycle, but even before he dismounted it, he heard:"Yes.Why will you now come to this place? You've become a big shot after joining the railway school, haven't you? "The barb was coming from Dikshit's mother. Braving it, he reached his friends, and replied to mother-in-chief in a matter-of-fact manner," I have to perform many additional tasks these days including supervising the shop for some hours. I really don't have much time left after school. Appreciate you must . . . ."

"You and sit at the counter? Did you say you supervise the shop? Tell this to some nit-wits and nincompoops. They'd believe it, not me." She insisted on this point and did not budge even an inch from her incredulity. If a chameleon was found tick-ticking synchronizing her speech she'd cite even its noise as affirmation of her statement.

He fell silent before this sarcasm but his friends rescued him from this situation allowing him to go where he was heading.

"He might be late for the school. His school isn't less than two kilometers away from this place. He must leave immediately." One of them said somewhat clumsily. He was sorry he couldn't convince mother-in-chief that he'd little time for the earlier kind of sittings at this place because he was really busy.

If he didn't give time to assist his father in the shop, the pressure was likely to fall upon his two younger brothers who were too small to think of anything other than school. If they were forced now to sit in the shop they might lose interest in school altogether after sometime. At their age, the first preference was play. According to Ratnakar's mother the question whether they were bright or not in studies was stupid and irrelevant. She clearly averred they were entitled to school as much as Ratnakar. Though his father differed with Ratnakar's mother on this point because he believed if one had to learn the ropes of the business one should better start learning them right from childhood.But he never made it a point of dispute because Ratnakar always came forward whenever there was a crowd of unmanageable customers in the shop. This happened generally on workshops' paydays or festivals.

Ratnakar had learnt to cut off from his friends on such occasions. Life continued in this manner for sometime. But the problem came when he joined a different school.

It was a surprise to find Sipra standing out in the open space before her house combing her unruly curly hair carelessly, when Ratnakar, leaving his main part of the house, was stepping towards his tin-roofed room. Previous to this event, he was laughing a bit loudly at some jokes with other members of his family. The happy smile was still playing on his lips when she winked at him. Before he could decide it was an inadvertent act on her part, she winked once more and turned her head with unwieldy loosened hair and a smile he never saw before. Thunderstruck, he stood a moment longer than was necessary or normal. She disappeared after the act or the confrontation. Two winks and a smile later, she wasn't the same person.

Ratnakar never thought of himself in the light of a hunted animal He was yet to form a response. His instinct told him that it was some kind of a trap. Trap or no, he must come out with an adequate answer. But what if she pushed her act further than this?

Her uncle Prahlad Dutta, who must be senior to him by 12 years, if not more, became an admirer of his reading caliber before becoming his fan and friend. But he believed in the creed of joie de vivre and did not appear to attach much importance to his state of unemployment. He talked volubly about games and sports and on any topic in general but on the issue of any school text book he simply shrank. He was delightfully ignorant about school books and teaching. Clearly, he was not competent in any manner to help his niece Sipra in her studies.

If there ever was a man with ubiquitous smiling face, it was Prahlad Dutta.. But, no mistake, he was as clever as fox, and as alert. He knew about Ratnakar's growing interest in Communism and the Communist Party of India.

"If you're attracted to the Communist Party of India temporarily because of your tender age," Prahlad said, "it's all right. But if you want to seriously involve yourself in it, you must try to know the reality, details and definitions of Communism. You must know, in a word, its basics."

"Yes. I believe I know enough about it to like it." Ratnakar replied."But what are you driving at? Please tell me."

"All right. Then let me put it this way. What is the full form of USSR?" Dutta asked.. " United States of Soviet Russia." Ratnakar's reply was unhesitant, without batting an eyelid.

Prahlad Dutta just laughed. Nothing could be more irritating to Ratnakar than this laughter coming from a man who was as far from CPI as near he was to it. What does he know of it to laugh in this manner? He felt insulted and humiliated.

Dutta stopped laughing, realizing his friend's hurt. "But you're wrong. The correct answer is Union of Soviet Socialist Republics. If you work on a wrong concept you'll end up in a wrong destination. And perhaps grief.. "

Ratnakar' faith in his understanding and in him got a crushing blow as the enormity of his mistake, ambiguity, confusion dawned on him. He learnt his lesson from a person he did not consider his equal in this particular area. The logic of the situation proved no person was unequal to him.

So far as the others of the circle he moved in were concerned it really didn't matter whether USSR was an abbreviation of United States of Soviet Russia or Union of Soviet Socialist Republics. It was enough if one had the humanity and sincerity to work for the good of the poor and the down-trodden people and dedicate one's energy to unite them for a change in the society. One couldn't be a communist, his leaders used to say, without loving the poor with their dirty dress and smell. But the jolt dealt by Prahlad Dutta had certainly thrown him out of complacency and made him aware of Dutta's power of keen observation and only increased his respect for him.

It was consequently unbelievable to think Sipra's unusual way of throwing her charms about or defiance of some outdated customs escaped his attention. Something was in the fire. Before she became an embarrassment to the family her parents took her to Jamshedpur and married her off. Duttas were a decent family and they did what was best in the situation. While other neighbours expressed happiness (and a certain relief) at the wonderfully correct solution of a family problem Ratnakar was confused. Was Sipra forced to leave her studies and sacrificed at the altar of some stupid pride and prejudice?

The answer to this question was perhaps hidden in future. Ratnakar was not qualified to sit in judgment over such events.

CHAPTER FIVE

Kadampur was passing through a horrific period of time in its career when nothing was right and everything was in a state of chaos. By this time the town, leaving aside the well-demarcated railway area with railway workshops and settlements and open spaces, had a municipality which existed only in name because it did nothing for drainage, roads, electrification; or for that matter, anything that benefited the citizens. But surely it proved its raison de etre in a different field: in collecting revenue in different heads from the captive people with threats of action if they failed to pay the levied money.

So far as the workers and common people were concerned, the town was a moneylenders' market. To say that it was a paradise for them would be picturesque, but more near the truth. Rice mill owners, oil mill owners and other kinds of hoarders had a field day. They could exploit, fleece the poor and do just anything without any fear of reprisal or punishment from any quarters. The tales of rickshaw drivers being underpaid or just being beaten for asking for more money were heard daily. Some ladies of richer families were not lagging far behind in fleecing the rickshawwallahs. Yes, you've rightly guessed. This was the Congress party's heyday when these exploiters could have anything on a platter including the head of an inconvenient protester.

With the lifting of the ban on the CPI, open political activities were made possible for it and Harinarayan Mishra and Biren Chakrabarty and Shanti 'da and some others opened a small office on the main road, School Road, of the town. They approached the common people to discuss their problems and enlist their sympathies; some shied away, some confided into them.

"How do you fit into this scene?"Banwarilal asked Ratnakar one day." You're still a student in school. But you give more time to the Party than to your studies."

Razzaque, who was a newcomer to Banwarilal's place but known to him otherwise because he met him elsewhere also, lent his support to Banwarilal and wondered,"Are you a Party worker or a student ?Tell me. You've become indistinguishable from a party worker because you're engaged in so many diverse activities of the Party. I think it's not fair for you; you're simply blocking your future."

Coming as it did from Razzaque who was a monument of sincerity and who would not utter a word unless it was coming from his heart, Ratnakar could not come out with an immediate response. However, he replied after a distinct pause: "You've done well to caution me. I was confused by the twin loyalties. From this time onward I assure you I'll give top priority to studies."

True to his assurance to his friends he minimized his contact with the Party by simply not going to the office in the evenings. Though some new faces could be seen occupying the bench in front of the table indicating Party's growing influence. Ratnakar's absence could not remain unnoticed for long by some senior members of the Party who felt concerned about him: Was he all right? Or, had some family problem troubled him ?

Harinarayan Mishra himself came to his house one day and called him. He was moving in the area on his bicycle making public contacts. Though he did not dismount the cycle because he did not have to as he was tall enough to keep his feet on the ground, he asked Ratnakar as soon as he came out: "Are you sick? What's wrong with you?"

"No", I replied promptly, "I'm all right, Mishra 'da. Who told you I'm ill?"

"You suddenly stopped coming to the Party office. You know we we're all concerned about you. If you have any problem we shall discuss about that. Why do you think we shall not share your problem? Come to the office in the evening."

And he went to the office in the evening. His problem was dissected on the table. The discussion was fruitful so far as it went. He would not be included in the programme of fund collection, procession and writing posters. The party had opened a new front——the student front. He was to look after it in the time left after his studies. It was a reasonable solution of the problem. The assurance given to his friends, alas, was better said than done in the ultimate analysis.

His life as a student of railway boys' high school, however, was distinct and separate from the Party connection. Ratnakar was so immersed in school activities while in school that no trace of Party could be found in him. He'd quite a set of jolly friends who enlivened his stay in the school. Harshad Rai,Anand P. Vyas,Narhari Das were average students coming from Gujarati stock but were great and splendid as friends and extremely cooperative even in other matters. In fact they studied together as a team at Ratnakar's place to prepare for

School Final Examination in 1955. Abdul Aziz, Shamim
and some others formed another group from Urdu section
who added dramatic touch to Ratnakar's school affairs.
His bond with them stood the test of time and proved
unbreakable even when they reached college. Looking
back at his school life Ratnakar had no cause to protest, to
rebel against anything because teaching there was a model
and benevolent discipline ruled. But to say that everything
was all right in the school would be a travesty of truth
because there was no doubt a perceptible undercurrent
of discontent and dissatisfaction among sections of staff
regarding imagined or real neglect of Hindi, or Urdu, or
Bengali section by the authorities. All this, however, was
subdued.

The picture of comparatively peaceful and satisfactory
condition of this school was soon going to be contrasted
with the stark and pitiable state of affairs of other schools
in the town. Disillusion, when it came, startled him.
It was after he took up the charge of student front after
a dramatic interlude. He had just sat for the school final
examination and was free from the tension. When he
was laughing at some jokes of his comrades in the office,
entered a group of gentlemen who introduced themselves
as guardians of a school the trouble at which sent them
running to this office for succour. They appeared agitated
and aggrieved about some matters having a direct bearing
on their wards. Since the space in the office was scarce,
some comrades vacated the benches to make room for the
newcomers and went out. But the guardians didn't have to
wait for long as Mishra 'da came within fifteen minutes of
their arrival. As soon as the issue was broached, Mishra
'da asked Ratnakar to sit on a chair beside him. Comrade
Mishra told them, after hearing their litany of grievances

against the headmaster, "This young man, Com. Ratnakar, will go to that school tomorrow. Ask your wards to meet him at the gate of the school half an hour before the school starts. He'll study problems first hand from the students. If necessary, Ratnakar will hold a meeting with these students in the evening at a separate place and prepare a charter of demands. It means he'll see the headmaster only day after tomorrow with necessary preparation."

One of the guardians said, "What if the headmaster refuses to see Ratnakar dubbing him a rank outsider. You don't know the HM. He considers himself too powerful."

"Then Ratnakar will organize students for agitation. He's a leader of Students' Federation. The HM will soon find out Ratnakar is not an outsider so far as the students and the organization are concerned."

The guardians apparently expected immediate action or solution. But this was not to be. That they got sympathetic hearing and assurance of movement ought to satisfy them, some of them realized before leaving the office.

The beginning had been made. The guardians and students started meeting him in the office or outside, even at home. Problems streamed into him not only of Kadampur's high schools but even from outside. Confining himself to Kadampur's educational institutions what he confronted there was frightening. One girls' high school had no arrangement of sanitation at all. Another girls' high school had something in the name of urinal but it was never cleaned since it was built. To use it was for them to court disease. The stink was enough to deter even the maddest . . .

Ratnakar was sitting at a friend's place when the subject of woman's place in Indian society came up.

Jeetendra commented," Isn't it a fact that in every family women are treated shabbily while Indian tradition and leaders talk of giving a very high place to woman in Indian society ?"

"If the headmistress of a high school is to be believed," Ratnakar breezed in," her school doesn't have a lavatory because the girls have mastered the art of self-denial: they don't need it and so there's no toilet facility there." He paused." This is perhaps the first ladder for them to go up to the seat of reverence in Indian society!"

Prem Singh jumped in, "This is exactly what Indian tradition is: hypocrisy. And we, believe me, monopolize in it."

CHAPTER SIX

The story of boys' high schools was no less frightening. There was no arrangement of drinking water in a large number of schools even during summer. In one instance, one Hindi high school teacher got so powerful that he arrogated to himself the authority to decide the promotion of a student from his present class to a higher class while the other teachers looked the other way. If one thought the examination or the marks obtained by the student that factored in his promotion, one couldn't be more grievously mistaken. The promotion was finalized on the basis whether a student had taken private tuition from the said almighty teacher. Nothing else mattered in it. But the secretary of another high school, Vinay Kumar Agrawal, who took Rs 500/—per new admission as a personal levy must take the cake for using an extremely ingenious method. He wouldn't collect money from the new entrant or the guardian. He'd simply ask the HM to send him the register of new entrants and ask him to pay Rs 50,000/—if the new admissions numbered 100 and Rs one lakh if the number went to 200.If any guardian protested, it would be against the HM's extortion. The secretary would remain safe. But if the HM failed to meet the secretary's demand, his administration would feel the full fury of his wrath. That the president, or the secretary, or the headmaster took bribe from a new assistant teacher before his or her appointment was taken for granted, with no questions raised. This was the shape of affairs in private schools during Congress regime.

But Ratnakar had thrown himself up against the powerful winds of exploitation. If he thought himself a revolutionary this was the time he realized how powerful and well-entrenched were the vested interests all around him and how small a fry he was.

How many mothers had Ratnakar? might sound an off-putting and embarrassing question to others but Ratnakar could take it upfront as he had no cause to live down a reality, in fact, a legacy, that was rich. But the question had a relevance in so far as it had a bearing on his mental make-up. He really had more than one mother at his formative stage. He remembered he called the other mother "badi maa", who lived with them albeit only for some time. For some time, because she left them before Ratnakar reached the age of distinguishing between two mothers. His mother was a modest woman of fair complexion, meek by nature, and slow as a talker."Badi maa "could shout and rant and words flew from her tongue like spears. After her departure Ratnakar was given to understand that it was she who always picked up some quarrel with his father because she wanted to live independently and alone. She was dark and came from an agriculturist family of a nearby locality in this part of Bengal. But Ratnakar with his elder sister and younger brother was quite happy with her because she had affection for them. After her departure from their house, she lived in a different part of the town in a thatched quarter and sold vegetables for a living at Gate Market.

"Who broke this glass jar? What, Ratnakar? I'll thrash you for causing this loss." His father was shouting. Ratnakar started running to escape from his father's indignation.

"Don't think I'm going to leave you. Whenever you come back I'll take your skin off."

These threats made Ratnakar flee to "badi maa ". His father was in so high a dudgeon that even after coming to know that he took shelter there he didn't make any immediate effort to take him back. Instead he declared Ratnakar would come back sooner or later when he wouldn't find anything to eat.

Ratnakar not only put himself in a mess but threw his "badi maa" also in trouble by his rash act. Clearly she was not prepared for this kind of situation. But she had enough of affection to give him what she had as food: watery stale rice and salt and onion and green chilly. In the morning, she would ask him to accompany her to the Gate Market where she sold vegetables. He'd sit on the mat with her and help her sell vegetables in the scorching heat of the Sun.

"You're sweating. Go; take some rest under the shade of that tree." She said to him pointing to a tree. She felt it was not proper for him to go through this troublesome experience but she also felt helpless before her fondness for him: she didn't want him to feel unwanted there. Asking him to go back would perhaps break her. But the reality of her existence forced her after a couple of days to take the boy back to his house. His return ended a chapter. By the time Ratnakar was admitted in a school (pathshala) for his first lessons the memory of "badi maa" began to fade in the face of newer demands of life.

Ratnakar visited at times Jagadish Rao at one of Number 1 quarters where he lived with his elder brother who was a driver of coal engine in the railways.

"Well, what happened? Start eating idalis. Or the coffee will grow cold." Jagadish said to Ratnakar.

"I was watching the scene of your mother fetching water from the public tap and sprinkling almost a quarter of it from the container on the way back before each step to purify the path." Ratnakar said tonelessly."That she retained this brahministic culture or prejudice till this old age is nothing short of a marvel."

"There's no arguing against it. Don't think about it."Jagadish had taken up his cup of coffee and started sipping it.

Dry, sour and salty powder—a kind of chatani—that went well with idalis was the specialty at his place. He started eating them along with sips of coffee.

His brother had to spend time sleeping if at home because the call to join duty might come any hour of the day or night, no matter if he was off-duty just half an hour ago. Loco-running staff was not only over-worked,it seemed, but also severely underpaid considering price index and health point. His rest could not be disturbed.

For small talks, they agreed, some other place.

When Ratnakar entered college it was following two-year term for I.A. and another two-year term for B.A. It had all three faculties up to degree level. Since he suffered too much mother-care by too many mothers in his earlier avatar he could breathe free and fresh air in it as it was co-educational meaning he could have an eyeful of compensation. It would also afford him the opportunity of organizing some of them, if not all, in his students' organization which was a greater and more serious task. Students' union election was round the corner and groups sitting by the college swimming pool situated at the centre were abuzz with election affairs. The newcomers, that is, the first year students, didn't have the faintest idea of what it was all about. Clearly, politics had yet to enter the arena. The first year students were groping in the dark and unless senior students came forward to enlighten them they might remain ignorant and not participate in the election at all. Each class had to choose representatives on the roll strength proportionately.

Ratnakar was sitting in the only canteen, outside the college, called Pulin da's cabin, with his close student friends. Rani Chatterjee was the first to speak:"I want to contest from first year science class. As girl students shy away from election, announcement of my name might encourage other girls to come forward."

"Yes. We want girls to participate in the election." Shamim said."But before we select them we must ascertain whether they are like-minded or not. The girls we offer candidatures must be progressive."

"But what's the measure of one's being progressive?" Surinder Kaur intervened, questioning.

Ratnakar said," That's what your job is: you must try to find out how strong a girl student is in her conviction."

"That's not done in a day." Surinder argued.

"You've clear four days. Persuade those who agree to write:"I agree to contest the election. "And sign it. This is necessary before we announce their names on the fifth day." Ratnakar declared.

CHAPTER SEVEN

J ayanta Naha, who was given the charge to oversee the students' election by the Party, suggested to Ratnakar that instead of discussing the nomination forms matter in the office it'd be better if he came to his house at Netaji Palli to finalize the issue which needed minute attention to eliminate any chance of rejection. Just one meeting with him at his place made Ratnakar intensely aware of Jayanta's superior intellect, and convinced him that this third year student knew all there was to understand about the election, and disabused his mind of some misconceptions. If there was any natural, born leader of students, he thought, it was Jayanta. Therefore he had no hesitation in conceding him the rightful place of a guide in the battle of students' election.

A mere 5feet 2 inches, nothing suited him better than a white dhoti and shirt which was no hindrance to his spirited movement. The young man of 22 who oozed a confidence about him that infected others suffered from a fault: he didn't know how to ride a cycle. He went to the college by rickshaw with a stopover at Sahu's shop for his paan (betel) beedas pack. Ratnakar struck an immediate friendship with him.

"Not all is well with the Party. Your selection of candidates might be disapproved by the Party". He started." This might happen at any time in the future."

"So?"

"It'd be in your interest to associate with me for complex situations. What you think a straightforward situation might be full of intricacies and ambiguities."Jayanta cautioned me "I have been through it many times ".

"Oh. Thank you Jayanta for giving me something to chew over." Ratnakar was astonished to learn that something was hidden in the simple deal of college affairs.

"I asked you to come to my place because I was genuinely interested in you as a future comrade and wanted you to know about the traps of your adversaries."

"Traps?"

"Yes. Traps."

"Well, now I don't understand you." Ratnakar felt frustrated

"Do you know what you did today—working hard,enlisting support, making the candidates agree to contest and sign the nomination papers—during the day is going to be undone by some people at night ?" Jayanta stopped.

"Are you telling me a fairy story or testing my intelligence? You haven't given any logical premises for this conclusion."Ratnakar's throat was dry.

"Your friends in the Congress camp would move at night and go to the parents of the vulnerable candidates you selected and persuade them to follow their reasoning. They'd tell them Ratnakar belongs to the Communist Party and their wards—sons or daughters'—association with him might prove dangerous for them in future. If the parents happen to be railway employees, the Congressmen'd tell them that their wards would find it hard to get Government jobs because of the existing rule of police verification in Government recruitment which practically means political verification. And they are the most threatening words to any parents. The result: The candidates influenced in this manner might withdraw their candidatures at the crucial time. "Jayanta was looking straight in his eyes.

There was a glass of water on a nearby table. Ratnakar looked at Jayanta and then at the glass. He went straight for the glass unable to control the urge for it and drank it in one gulp.

"If some guardians brushed aside the Congressmen's loaded advice," Jayanta continued, "They had another thing coming. The IB—shorter form of Intelligence Branch. Some IB people would pay a visit to the concerned railway employees to caution them that their wards and they themselves might come to harm if their wards don't disassociate with the communistic activities. This could be an attempt to make the threat real and it works ninety times out of a hundred."

Jayanta was not joking. What he wanted was Ratnakar should be more careful and keep his flock under constant vigil and let not a crack set in it.

Both Rani Chatterjee who was milky white and Shreya Bhowmik who was a shade dark in appearance worked as a team, and moved among the students like two ditties. The Juno's sisters were right here. There was no question coming from different classes they did not know the answer of. They chatted with them on the lawns of the college and in class rooms. In fact, it appeared at times that students in small groups just awaited them. Clearly, they left no stones unturned to see their candidates victorious. They sweated as profusely as Ratnakar did to shatter the opponents' camp. Sometimes Rani and Shreya took the platform of the classes with or without the permission of the authority because the students wanted them to speak from the podium. This left no doubt about students' genuine enthusiasm for them.

But the college had also night shift running commerce classes where a huge number of students studied. This was a no-go zone for Rani Chatterjee and Shreya Bhowmik for obvious reasons. And the night classes were dominated by the opponent's camp

Though the election was fought on non-political lines, its political overtone gradually became apparent as the election drew near.

Ratnakar and his friends had to draw a different strategy for night section commerce students who mostly consisted of railway employees or elderly dropouts. That Ratnakar's opponents were in a comfortable position here did not need elaboration. It was a given. If Ratnakar wanted to make a dent here he must establish his competence as a convincing speaker because the audience of elders was sufficiently experienced to judge him. Before they shifted their allegiance they must be satisfied that Ratnakar and his friends could deliver the goods. Ratnakar knew for this he had to depend entirely on his own resources. Where English oratorical skill alone worked Jayanta was no help.

But there was a perceptible undercurrent movement beneath the surface of full swing election activities. It was a parallel exploration of human relations which suggested who liked whom, when and where. It could be just a glance which couldn't go much beyond meeting of eyes.

In some cases there might be sound and fury that signified nothing. In knowing looks and smiles of boys and girls one could detect a warm respect for each other. Ratnakar had nothing to do with the budding real or fake romances because he had a mission to accomplish from which he could not flinch.

But one thing was troubling him. Rani Chatterjee and Shreya Bhowmik had already become well-known faces in the college, leaders in their own right, ditties and surprises. Stories of some boys falling in love with them were brought to Ratnakar's notice who immediately scotched them. What Ratnakar's problem was that they were going beyond his control. He did not want them to be part of romantic stories doing the subdued rounds of the college. At least till elections.

Who else but Jayanta Naha had the key to solve the problem currently faced by Ratnakar?

"Rani and Shreya have done an excellent job of winning the hearts of majority of students. This will show in the election results."Jayanta said.

"If they keep away from the college for some romantic escapades at the crucial time for a day or two, we might have to eat dust." Ratnakar expressed his apprehension.

"Don't worry about that. Nothing is likely to happen till the election, in their love—front. I'm saying this on the basis of sufficient information I gathered about the two episodes." Jayanta paused only to change his position on the chair."But what about the night shift?"

"I believe I've been able to make some dent there. How much, I can't say." Ratnakar's tone was assuring.

"If we win even one third of seats there, students' union will be ours." Jayanta was smiling.

CHAPTER EIGHT

He, who can, does. He, who cannot, teaches.
—GBShaw, Man and Superman

There was no question about any ambiguity in the students' union constitution: the contradiction that was written into it stared all in the face. The election of the vice-president was direct in the sense all the classes of day and night shifts were considered one unit unlike the elections of General secretary, common room secretary and others who were elected from among the winning class-representatives on the basis of majority. There was an inbuilt mechanism—and that's the crux of the matter—of loopholes which could give birth to sinister plots in the method of this vice-presidential election : The provision was that there should be one room and one ballot box for all the 1500 to eighteen hundred students from both shifts with the time fixed between 3pm and 8pm—5 hours. This was a mockery of democratic rights to vote because 1500 students could not complete the processes of voting which included verification of their dues clearance certificates within the specified time. Clearly this was aimed at excluding girls from voting as they generally left the college after 4 pm. It was heavily weighed in favour of the night class students who were generally railway employees and were afraid of showing anti-administration stance in any matter. It needed superhuman endeavour and time, both of which were in short supply, to change their mind-set.

Ratnakar was considering the issue over and over again but no solution to it presented itself to his mind which was highly agitated. Though his Students' Federation had won thumping majority in class representative's elections and were heading towards distributing portfolios among themselves, the idea of the presence of a non-conformist vice-president in meetings was disconcerting.

With some such thoughts he was walking towards Pulin da's cabin hoping to meet some friends there. Just then there was a thunder in the sky and he became aware of the darkening clouds. He looked at the sky to gauge its mood. If he didn't walk faster rains might catch him before he made it to the cabin. He heaved a sigh of relief as the shower was a moment too late for it to wet him.

Ratnakar saw Mohammad Shamim sipping his cup of tea and Surinder Kaur biting into samosa in the last bench of the bistro.Before he took the first step towards them he found Rani and Shreya emerging from nowhere, rushing towards him and shaking his hands effusively which left him stunned for a moment. It was a measure of their enthusiasm over the thunderous victory.

"Ratnakar 'da, congratulations."Both of them expressed simultaneously. Their gestures though did not need the voicing by words—they were eloquent enough . . . It was unforgettable.

They were meeting here for the first time after the results were declared yesterday night when no girl candidates were present though they were represented by their authorized agents.

"You deserve a treat for making this victory spectacular." Ratnakar couldn't restrain his warmth and happiness for them. "What'd you like to have? Sweets or samosas?"He was laughing.

"If you really want to give us a treat," Shreya said mischievously," we'd prefer Modern Restaurant to any other place to celebrate it."The place was famous for gourmets' delights.

"That's done." Ratnakar replied. "When?"

"Tomorrow."

They moved towards an empty table in this mutual congratulatory and enthusiastic mood that knew no end. That this occasion was for celebration was evident from each warm gesture they made, from each carefree word they spoke. Some lines could remain in the time of sand.

After the initial euphoria of victory was over, the students' union started functioning leisurely with its programmed events and Ratnakar's presence in them was formal and just where necessary. Now it wasn't the college affairs, but the Party work that became important to him. There was no doubt that the Party stood still on the legs of Harinarayan Mishra who organized it, worked tirelessly for it and inspired others to work for the down-trodden people. But the Party's area was severely limited ; it couldn't work openly among railway men and in the railway area, rail being a Central establishment. What was left of Kadampur needed an imaginative and intellectual approach to reach the hearts of the common people. The space was admirably filled by Naveen Mitra, a later recruit, who knew how to make a poster striking, what to write, and how to make it beautiful. Hindi leaflets (and occasionally English too) were left to the care of Ratnakar while the main contents were jotted down by Com. Mishra and Naveen Mitra.

In the extended meetings where he was invited, Ratnakar felt Durgapada Ghosh took more time to present his views than others after Com Mishra submitted the reports and suggestions. Though Naveen Mitra spoke less than others his points always made the impact.

Ratnakar tried to absorb Marxism as much as possible from books and from practical measures in situational contexts in meetings. His mind struggled to find out whether this was merely an ideal in books or something achievable in this material world. The attempt led him to feel a certain gap somewhere. The people who were at the receiving end of exploitation had yet to identify their friends and enemies because they believed the present condition was their destiny which could not be altered. Clearly the dusty town needed an imaginative and scientific approach which could put its people on the road to struggle, to revolutionary materialism. But with only one chemical factory outside the railway zone, where four hundred hands worked, Kadampur wasn't the most ideal place to start a Communist party branch. But could one choose the people? You had to begin with what you had.

Beedi factories, small steel factories, oil mills and such others were the places where trade union activities could be started. All first attempts by the communists at these units were strongly resisted and frustrated by the owners. Naturally only where the workers were prepared trade unions were formed. The progress was slow; indeed very slow. What sustained the Party at that time were sheer ideology of Marxism-Leninism and the entry of persons like Naveen Mitra, Durgapada Ghosh, Jagannath Rao and Gurubux Singh who were not only strong-willed but sincere to the core.

"That oil mill owner did not allow me to hold a meeting at his premises," Durgadapada was one day narrating his experience with the owner to some comrades in the office, "even though I was called there by the workers."

"What'd you do then?"One of the comrades asked him.

"I'm going to fix up a place right now where I can hold meeting with workers. I've two places in mind near the mill." Durgapada's anger at the frustrating experience was obvious. A moment later he laughed." Do you know what Engels said about the exploiting class. To quote him;" As soon as our Party is in possession of power it has simply to expropriate the big landed proprietors and manufacturers in industry."

"But he's too small a fry to need this kind of treatment." Naveen Mitra joked.

What would Ratnakar do? He made entry into the second year arts class without going through any texts except for some notes he jotted down in the few classes he attended. If he had to pass the I.A. examination he had to attend regularly and do what the other students do. This was a tall order.

The year was 1956. The time 2 pm. He was with Md. Shamim, Rani Chatterjee and Shreya Bhomik in Pulin 'da's cabin, savouring his two-period long leisure in a mood of abandon. The little episodes of jokes that Shreya narrated made them laugh boisterously. The session could go on. But Jayanta's sudden entry in the scene seemed to give it a jolt. He took Ratnakar to a side, and spoke almost in whispers to him, "You must immediately start for the

Party office. You're an invitee in this meeting. The railway workers' sudden tool down strike is the subject."

"But . . ."Ratnakar could not complete the sentence.

"No buts. This is an extremely important issue." Jayanta said, "I want you to be there. I'm going there by rickshaw you fetch your cycle . . ."He went away leaving him nonplussed

Ratnakar left his friends even without taking a goodbye, leaving them wondering. Such was the urgency.

CHAPTER NINE

The out-fiending chaos in the railway workshop on April 12, 1956 was unparalleled in its annals because the day had witnessed the thrashing of the riveters' and brushers' shops' workers in a barbarous manner by the railway's armed guards when they were protesting against the administration's negligence and callousness which resulted in the crushing of a worker by a machine while he was performing the allotted duties. The death was caused entirely due to the railway's fault. The job in both the shops involved personal risk and the demands for protective aids though raised in proper fora had never been addressed. They were simply brushed aside. The passion had to reach a boiling point and it did with the death of the victim of the accident on the spot.

The protest by the victim's co-workers which took the form of tool-down strike was spontaneous. But so was the action of the railway's armed guards—instantaneous. It's they who went berserk hitting, banging, striking the workers in a wild manner.

But the story of this inhuman torture filtering through the gates spread like wildfire in the homes and quarters of the wounded workers. Some of the womenfolk,half in anger and half in madness, decided to make a forced entry into the workshop surprising the watchmen, with broomsticks and whatever they could lay their hands upon,to protect their men folk from the armed guards' attack. This certainly changed the scene inside the two workshops. The women fighting this battle made the rest of the workers join the tools down strike.

When the workers did not turn up for work the following day also, the railway administration, instead of thinking on the lines of redress of their demands, chose to be vindictive and involved the State and police with a view to arresting the strike leaders and all. The idea was to instill a sense of fear and terror among them so that they surrendered and joined the work. Since both the riveters' shop and the brushers' shop had an overwhelming number of Telugu hands and the accident involved a Telugu worker, the railway administration in a calculated manner spread the rumour that Bengalis were not participating in this strike. Dividing the working class community to weaken the morale of the strikers was the trick it played.

Ratnakar was sitting on the grass of Victoria ground as usual with his friends Chalpati, Awasthi, Mani, Ranga, Gajwe for his evening session, discussing literature and recent activities of some social organizations It was not known who suggested the idea of starting a library but the subject was taking a serious form when Papa Rao,who catered to their tea and snacks requirements there,came rushing to them and spoke to Chalpati rapidly something in Telugu as if he was in some kind of a hurry. Chalpati nodded in agreement and slowly stood up,saying," We should break the meeting. Papa informed me that two police vans were standing nearby which meant the police could surround the ground any moment for indiscriminate arrests. His advice was for us to disperse immediately." Though they dispersed in twos they could hear, without turning back, someone shouting at the policemen, who had already pounced upon a group of sitting young men," I'm not a railway worker. I'm Chinna, a shopkeeper at Gatarpara."

"But your name is Chinna?"

"Yes, so what?"The man continued to shout.

He was dragged to the waiting police van. The police got instruction from the local Congress boss to arrest only Telugus because he knew how to tackle such situations. But the workers' union declared its all-out support to the strike foiling their heinous attempt to divide the workers in Bengali and Telugu camps.

Earlier, the same day in the afternoon, Ratnakar attended the Party meeting where the workshop's tools down strike was discussed. There was a girl who was found usually sitting on a bench or carpet doing something or the other whenever he went to the office. It was her ubiquitous presence that was remarkable. But he never saw her attending a meeting. Therefore he was surprised to find her participating in this important meeting. In the middle of it, Ratnakar said: "Since the railway is a Central Government establishment, the employees should have followed rules of serving prior notice to the administration for its action—tools down, or strike, or whatever. Immediate protest over death is understandable. This reaction is human. But stoppage of work is going a bit too far."

Mishra was furious."You know nothing about it. Do you know that the demands for protective aids in the two shops had been outstanding for a very long time and the administration was on notice already for the three tragedies that occurred earlier? Human patience had reached the end with this cruelty of the rail."

Another comrade in support of Com.Mishra said," Did the rail respect or accept any rules in this matter? Why did it not act on the justified demands of the workers so far? Workers have lost their limbs and lives. To call it a wild cat strike, after four tragedies, is uncivilized on its part. This is the limit of exploitation."

"Frankly I did not know these details."Ratnakar clarified." But if I was ignorant about the history of railway's breaking of rules and its exploitation the Party is responsible for it. We never discussed the railway matter. Now that you've brought out certain facts I feel the rail is guilty."

"The rail issues were never considered here because they are beyond the province of this Party.' Naveen Mitra interjected."The rail being a national industry is looked after by trade unions, recognized or otherwise."

"If the workers had rebelled against it, throwing the rules out, they still must be" Mishra continued, "supported. When they are being hit hard the Communist Party could not remain mere spectators to this sight. They must be by the side of the workers even when they might be technically wrong."

Harinarayan Mishra jumped into the charged atmosphere and got arrested immediately near the workshop gate. It was the other Party men who worked tirelessly when he was in jail with other railway workers.

But, Biren Chakrabarty was annoyed with the way Com Mishra got himself arrested near the workshop gate addressing a group of people shouting Party's support for the strikers' cause. He could have avoided this arrest by skipping that address near the gate which was known to be under constant vigil by the police. Why did he choose to be an easy target was his searching question. He was required more outside to give leadership than inside jail with the arrested workers to do nothing. Apparently, there were no takers of Biren Charabarty's view. Or so it seemed.

With the strikers in no mood to yield to the State and railway administration's unrelenting torture and the rail playing a game of outsmarting the strikers by creating black legs among them, the situation was getting from bad to worse.

The continuing night raids forced the men folk to leave their quarters to sleep in the unfrequented open spaces. Just anywhere but their homes. Enraged at not finding the workers in their quarters the police turned to attacking the womenfolk in vengeance. And this snowballed into a conflict of an unknown dimension. The women started to fight back police with broomsticks, chilli powder with a ferocity not heard before. This exhibition of women's power, with their backs to the wall, compelled the attackers to halt their operation, at least temporarily. But the rail's armoury was not exactly short of unnerving ideas. It tried to put pressure on them by giving notice to vacate quarters. The cup of woes was still to be filled for them.

The district committee which got daily brief of the development here asked the State leadership to act immediately.

Blacklegs joining the work were the last straw on the camel's back. The strikers thrashed them wherever they found them. A driver taking a train from Midnapur carrying black legs, among others, was dragged down from the engine near Victoria ground halt. It was started and left to run driverless up to the dead-end of the platform where it struck and stopped. The story of driverless train which was splashed in newspapers as world class news since then became a part of the strike lore.

Since police raids were in the air, the Communist Party had to take extreme caution in respect of supporting the strikers with the few members and sympathizers it had. They must avoid arrest as far as possible to continue holding area meetings and pasting posters.

"Are Hindi posters ready?" Shouted Durgapada Ghosh at Jagannath Rao.

"Not only Hindi but Telugu posters also have been put in that bundle." Jagannath replied gravely.

"Where is Ratnakar? Hasn't he turned up yet with the paste?"Durgapada controlled his voice but his impatience was evident.

"Making gum takes time."Naveen Mitra intervened."He'd buy flour, find a hotel's oven. I think he must be on his way back now."

"Durga 'da, why this impatience? After all, we're not hitting the road before 10 pm." Jagannath said cautiously, and wondered loudly, "But where is your ladder?"

Durgapada started laughing loudly. His mood changed."So you're getting back at me."He continued his laughter which made the atmosphere light.

"I've hidden the stair in a safe place."Durgapada said." I'll take it on our way out to postering. Just see it."

It was near a particular corner of the printing press wall where Durgapada was sticking poster when he faced resistance from a group of cinema workers who considered his act as an encroachment on their reserved space. They said no to Durgadpada and it could have taken an ugly turn of quarrel had not Naveen Mitra intervened, reasoning with them that it's they who'd come to their aid in their need, and soon start a union in their cinema as some of their colleagues were already in touch with them. Some of them did understand the importance of these posters after what Naveen Mitra told them, and agreed, for the time being, to let them go ahead pasting posters at their reserved spot.

As it happened in such cases—three steps forward, two steps backward—the workers had to join the workshop and the railway had to give some assurance of not victimizing strikers, except some who it considered too militant for it or otherwise dangerous, and providing masks and other protective aids to those performing risky duties, after the district and central leadership of the Party brought the pictures of the rail's glaring inhuman torture to the national focus. The strike drew out two things into the open : One was the stark reality of blacklegs who could not be wished away ; the other was the springing up of the best emotions among them for one another, one helping the other with money and food without thinking of what lay in store for him for the next day.

Harinarayan Mishra became overnight the most popular name. Even while in jail, stories of his valour spread in the small town of Kadampur. Clearly, a change was overtaking the previous mind-set in the horizon. When finally Com. Mishra and others were released from jail, the Communist Party office started buzzing with activities and common people.

Ratnakar, like some others had the opportunity of seeing closely district and State leaders during the short struggle, underground and open. Their dedication to the cause had dispelled any doubt that he might have had about the Party. He felt he must uphold the struggle for working class and peasantry. Yes, this strike decided for him what he should do. He applied for membership of the Party.

On May Day 1956 he was baptized in the Party as a member along with some others in the presence of Comrades S.Sengupta, Rabi Mitra,Deben Das and of course K.Bhowmik who was the district secretary in the Nimtalla Chowk Party office, and given a red card.

CHAPTER TEN

A sulking Rani was sore that she was refused a book on the ground that she already had two books issued in her name by the college librarian. If the library was there to help and encourage students to study more, denying her the book she wanted flew in its face. But the librarian spoke of the rules of lending books,and asked her to return the two books first if she wanted two other books to read. Of course, she realized the issue was beyond argument. And yet . . .

She had ordered a coffee instead of her usual cup of tea in Pulin da's cabin and decided to stay there for all day when she should be attending a meeting in the Students' Union office. Was this a way of showing her disapproval and anger to anyone who was hearing, or seeing or caring for her? For whom her bell tolled?

The Union meeting was discussing very important issues that were agitating the minds of the students who felt crassly ignored and just taken for a ride. They were demanding new playthings in the common room and approving for holding an overdue social function. The charge was getting strident that the office bearers of this Union were a bunch of dumb heads and unfits.

What was making her so unsympathetic, unfeeling, and stony to the Union for which she was ready to forgo anything not long ago? Had the librarian's refusal of a book to her anything to do with her present state of mind? One could go on guessing but the fact of life pointed to her heart. There was something broken there. Ruptured. The boy she loved had stopped coming to the college for last three weeks. All her efforts to trace him failed so far. For all practical purposes he became incommunicado. Clearly, it was this that had taken a toll on her. This was the clue to her disturbed mind, to her behavioral change, to her chaotic ways.

Shreya, who was attending the meeting, felt the stab of her absence and made excuses to leave it halfway through to find her and to talk to her. The moment Rani saw Shreya entering the cabin she felt an uncontrollable urge to weep on her shoulders. Shreya knew instinctively what was coming up next as she came closer to her and put her finger on her lips. "Don't show your tears here, my sweet girl." She whispered," This is a public place. We can talk about Samir somewhere else."

When Rani was drying her pearly eyes Shreya put her hands on her shoulders in a gesture of transmitting power and solidity.

"We can jointly solve the problem called Samir."Shreya said," I feel it needs more intellectual than any emotional exercise."

"The problem isn't here." Rani responded dryly." or at any other known place. Samir has disappeared from the scene without leaving any trace. Ergo; you don't solve a problem if it's not there. Can you?"

The service boy came and put two coffees on the table which just then was a welcome distraction.

"Your absenting from the meeting wasn't a wise thing in the circumstances obtaining just now. It was a very important meeting considering the excited students.'Shreya commented."The meeting would resolve to buy new play materials for common room and to invite a galaxy of singers and other artistes on the day of annual prize distribution."

"You should've stayed till the end of the meeting." Rani promptly replied, feeling concerned.

"Well, I found a way to get recorded my vote for the two items before I came out to find you."Shreya explained.

They started sipping coffee in silence for some minutes. Rani appeared to be recovering from her mood of despondency but relaxed she still was not.

"What about Dinesh?"Rani asked her in subdued tone.

Shreya blushed and her girlishness expressed her feeling for Dinesh. But she was not prepared for it as she was engrossed in Rani's pain and anxiety so long.

"Well," Shreya couldn't suppress a smile. "he's doing fine. He wrote a load of trash and called it his poetry of love. You can't imagine how boring he could be with that."

"But Dinesh is doing something terrible if what you say is true. Don't blame him for something he did not intend because boring you would be the last thing on his mind." Rani went on."Think of the time he must have spent going through the experience of putting his love in meters."

"It's repetition of the same phrases in all his poems that gets me."Shreya seemed to be lost in this heart-to-heart talk with her friend." Why can't he feel that poetry, or for that matter love, is not static?"

"Teach him that." Rani squeezed her shoulder a bit hard while speaking.

Shreya opened her mouth to reply but before any words came out she had sighted Ratnakar stepping into the cabin which had the effect of stopping her in the middle and looking thoughtful.

Ratnakar, who initially decided not to go to their table to express his displeasure at their willful and stupid absence from the meeting, walked to them reluctantly because that's the way the cookie crumbles.. It's only when he made himself completely comfortable in silence on their facing bench that he came out: "What makes you think that playing truancy is a much greater intellectual activity than attending the meeting and facing questions?'

Rani was silent. Shreya replied,"Ratnakar 'da, listen. She had a sudden bout of headache. She could have become a greater problem for all of you attending the meeting than what her resting here represents. There are some girly problems which you must realize make them stay away from meetings."

"Though what you said is all Greek to me,"Ratnakar said as he realized there might be some weighty reason for their truancy which they were not disclosing right now," I'd go by your explanation. Now no more of it. You can order a coffee for me."

It had started raining outside in the meanwhile and the splatter of big drops on the tin roof of a nearby shop gave enough signal that it meant to be relentless for quite some time. In silence they were introspecting their respective minds in this unsought confinement. Ratnakar's search of the minds of the two girls led him to his own loneliness. He desperately wanted the rain to stop immediately so that he could come out of this suffocating detention. He knew he couldn't be a denizen of the worlds where Rani and Shreya moved. The rain did not oblige Ratnakar. With the hot coffee placed near his hand he came back with a slow jolt to the surrounding reality, to the crowd of students in the cabin. He looked back only to find a girl, still in skirts, suggesting that she might be a first year student who had still to shed her school mindset, looking at him intently. Slowly he turned his face. Rani and Shreya were smiling.

Looking at Rani, Shreya asked her suddenly, "Have you ever eaten a live fish ?"

"Let me think . . . ."

"It's not about thinking. It's all about remembering."

"Why don't you place orders for a mutton-chop . . . er . . . mutton-chops for all of us in the meanwhile till she remembers. Or stop beating about the bush."Ratnakar permitted himself a smile

"That I will."

"What?"Ratnakar was both anxious and surprised.

"Place orders for mutton chops and what."And Shreya transformed this rainy day into a delicious occasion for all of them.

The rain outside was incessant. The atmosphere inside the cabin had now become stuffy, what with smoke coming in unshapely curls from cigarettes and noise. From where he was sitting he could see a lonely plant of rose through the window being beaten mercilessly by the raging rain. He hoped, as he was a hoper that flowers would come out again in all their shapeliness after a time. But is human life like this? He began to think. In a few months' time he had to face the final examination of Intermediate Arts for which his preparation, to say the least, was almost non-existent. Dropping the exam would not mean a breather for him but a signal for the end of his academic career which he could not afford. Life is not just a coffee here and mutton chop there but a much more serious business. Shorn of verbiage; you needed a job to live.

Rani and Shreya could afford to live in their separate worlds because, in the first place, they were brilliant students having no fear of exam, and secondly, they had the assurance from their would-be equally good life-partners. If Ratnakar had to shine in life he had to do something different from what he had been doing in academic front.

CHAPTER ELEVEN

Everybody perhaps knows to his (in a gender-neutral sense) cost that Time has a sense of humour. So long as it happens to others it looks funny. When Ratnakar made a decision to prepare for the final I. A. examination the meaning was unambiguous that he had to cease all political activities forthwith to implement it. An examination worked out to concentration on studies for a definite purpose. Unless he wanted to make a farce of it. But he was face-to-face with one of the greatest moral problems in his life. The year, not to forget, was 1957. The general election was to be held just two weeks before his IA final examination of Calcutta University commenced. He was in a dilemma. If he attached more importance to his appearing at the exam with the required readiness as a careerist than to the great ideological war which the election symbolized, then he would be showing his disloyalty to the ideology and shirking responsibility at an hour when the political situation couldn't be more favourable to the CPI for election.

A very big section of railway workers were disgusted with the Congress party and were raring to teach it a lesson, should they get the opportunity, for beating them and humiliating their womenfolk during the forced 1956 strike. It appeared that the Party could after all come out victorious if it used all its resources because the winning factor of common people's motivation was unmistakably evident. Could Ratnakar leave the Party alone at this hour and consider his career a better option? The situation wasn't exactly funny for him.

Though, put in a to-do or not-to-do predicament, he wavered for a moment but just. Ultimately, he decided in favor of working for the Party in the election forgoing his studies. With the excitement of election reaching a crescendo he could n't possibly remain a fence-sitter even if he wanted to. If the society had to be changed, it was a well-recognized axiom, collective sacrifice was made somewhere. Nobody could guess that he had recently undergone a mental struggle to devote fulltime to the Party because everybody thought that Ratnakar was doing just what was expected of him because it was taboo to discuss one's personal matters like exam particularly when the assembly election had already knocked on the door. No quarters would be given, he knew, to any excuse for one's slackening the effort at this stage.

Com. Mishra's comment when Ratnakar applied for membership of the Party and earned it in 1956 was:' You and Jagannath Rao started working for the Party at about the same time but he decided to be its member one year earlier than you did. This is because you came from a petty bourgeois family and he from a working class one. The difference in background explains this phenomenon.' If his present state of mind was due to this background, he couldn't help it.

But what was the Party like in 1957? The membership of the Party did not exceed even twelve leaving aside the railway which never was a part of the open Party. But the gap was well compensated for by a large list of Party sympathizers and supporters coming from all walks of life.

In addition, the CPI had a groundswell of support both in the railway and municipal areas which was conspicuous in large gatherings who flocked at street-corner meetings held to canvass vote for Com. Harinarayan Mishra. Com. Mishra's popularity was at its nadir,especially among Telugu-speaking people who constituted a substantial section of voters. They had not forgotten that it was Com. Mishra who jumped in their honour and trade struggle in1956 against the rail administration's and State police torture. They also remembered the other trade unions who came to their rescue and stood by them in their hour of need. Obviously this was the time for them to repay their gratitude But the Congress party had a solid base among the people and it could be a grave error of judgement if one thought that one event could change their ingrained outlook.

If the fledgling CPI found itself unable to cope with the electoral enquiries of its rising number of supporters spread over a wide area of Kadampur assembly constituency comprising railway and municipal areas it did not cause surprise. Even though this was the second general election after the promulgation of the Indian Constitution, the significance of voters' list, polling booth centres, voters' slip was yet to dawn on a large section of the people. The terms had a mystique about them which appeared to voters riddles. Some interested and inspired people did rush to the Party office to search their names in the voters' list. As against this there were thousands others who needed to be approached and enlightened. Clearly the job was technical and required hundreds of trained cadres to tell voters which specific polling centres they had to go and what slip of paper to carry which, after being verified by the polling officers, would enable them to vote by ballot paper. The time was short and the task was huge, and to describe it thus was an understatement.

The Party surely inspired its trade union wings and some teachers and students to take the responsibility of looking after the voters' list and what it implied.

Nabeen Mitra was heard saying loudly to Com. Mishra in the crowded Party office :"Mishra da, it's time you go to the State Party office to seek their help in the matter of training of election's technical aspects."

"But I'm jammed with so many programmes of meetings, home-sittings and collection of fund." Mishra da replied." My diary for seven days leaves no time for it."

"Then I should be authorized to go there to seek their help because election would become problematic and meaningless without this knowledge for our workers." Nabeen Mitra said

It appeared Mishra da ignored this part of election work so long in the din of euphonious slogans and meetings. He suddenly realized that voters' support was not enough. They should also be enabled to vote intelligently.

Realizing the significance of Mitra's concern, Mishra da laughed and said placatingly, "Why didn't you tell me about it earlier? I'm going to Calcutta tomorrow."

Then it used to take 4 hours or more to reach Calcutta by passenger trains from Kadampur. Those were the days of coal-driven engines.

Ratnakar was assigned the task of looking after Utkal High School polling centre which had four booths with voters' lists of four different areas containing nearly four thousand voters. Having been made in-charge of this polling centre by the Party it devolved on him to recruit dependable and tested persons to man the polling booths as official agents of the candidate inside the booths on polling day, and also to see that the lists were thoroughly explored which translated to personally visiting the voters' houses or quarters to verify the list. No doubt, the Party had given him half a dozen well experienced men to work under his supervision while the enormity of the job needed at least 20 such persons. Clearly, it was left to him to fill the gap. For a person who was till recently thinking in terms of devoting his time to study for the final exam, this end was truly paradoxical if not tragi-comic. Group meetings had to be held to fix dates and times for scrutiny of lists, for collection of money because working throughout the day and part of the night involved consumption of tea and snacks. It was a different matter that his sincere and spurred friends had their own pocket money for the purpose relieving him of this kind of tax-net. Imagine a picture of Ratnakar with a lantern in one hand and a voters' list in another moving in Jaihind Nagar in the evenings to verify the voters' identity. If he felt disconcerted at times it was equally true that he sensed most of the time being driven and inspired by an undying ideology. Moreover, he had two friends, with lanterns and lists, as company in those evenings which was sufficiently invigorating.

It was a pitiable situation because where hundreds of workers were required the Party could muster only 70 to do investigation. Nothing could be more absurd that despite evidence of a sympathetic wave for the Party in general and com. Harinarayan Mishra in particular, the Party failed to reach most voters at their homes. It was therefore found all the more necessary to construct on the day of election small booths one hundred yards away, to follow the rule, from the polling centres to help the voters with slips of identity indicating their name, age, sex, etc. But money was needed for even this kind of improvised structure with a table. Since the Party did not have much money for this kind of expenses on the day of election,the enthused workers came forward to smilingly bear the cost of the day. Such was the people's mood in 1957 election.

CHAPTER TWELVE

'Where had you been for the last whole week?'. Madhav asked Ratnakar somewhat sharply even before he stood the cycle a yard away from the group sitting on the worn-out not-so-green-grass of Victoria Ground.

'Don't you know?' Dubey intruded mockingly,' he was busy doing election work.'

'My foot! Has he taken the responsibility of the whole election for the Party? Aren't there others?'Madhav expressed his displeasure at Ratnakar's attempt to bite off more than he could chew in the election.

When Ratnakar was preparing to answer them so as to put them at ease, after some readjustment was made in the circle for him to sit on the ground, Chalpati began saying slowly,'Actually we felt concerned when reports reached us you were working like a whole-timer of the Party,neglecting studies,food,and health. Your absence from this meeting-place for a long period has naturally caused us some anxiety. We shall have nothing to say if you moderate your task.'

This group consisted of persons who were senior to him by 10 years or more and had only the best in their hearts for him.

'I'm giving most of my time to the Party because I feel Mishra 'da could win the election, the public mood being in our favour. It could turn out to be a victory of the working class. A change in future politics may be expected thereafter.' Ratnakar tried to justify his overdrive.

'Nonsense.Tsk, tsk, tsk What makes you think your Party will win 'Mani asked him a straight question.

'Because of 1956 strike. Because of the outraged feelings of a community. Because of Telugu victimization. In addition to the ever deteriorating economic condition of the people.'Ratnakar wanted to be short since Mani was a highly educated person, not needing a long answer where fewer words sufficed.

'This is what you think.' Mani said.' The basic flaw in you logic is that you ignore the fact that Kadampur workshop is a Central government organization which has service conduct rules. The workers—whether Telugus,Bengalis or others—know that if they are branded as communist supporters—which they will be if they vote the CPI to victory—they might have to face some kind of punitive action. Common sense dictates they wouldn't choose a harmful course.'

'But you belittle the fact that workers are in a mood to get even with the Congress and the railway administration,come what may. Nothing short of revenge for 1956 torture is what they want.' Though Ratnakar said this he was aware that Mani had rightly pointed out the weaknesses in his structure of syllogism.

'But this is 1957. 1956 is dead and buried.' Mani was in a mood to argue, and he seemed to be winning on points.'Majority of the workers who bore the brunt of 1956 administrative attacks might have either forgotten it or found reasons to make compromises. They may not be as aggressively anti-administration—or anti-Congress as you would like to have it—as they were in 1956.'

"You've a point there.'Ratnakar said.'But since we're in daily contact with a wide spectrum of people we know they haven't forgotten the wound inflicted by the rail administration in 1956 the scar of which is still visible in their eyes and in their contempt for what the rules stand for. '

'Do you mean to say the Congress is ignorant of what's going on among the workers? Or is it your presumption that it's dumb?' Mani put the razor-sharp questions.

'The Congress is neither ignorant of the workers' mood nor is it sitting idle. But its choice is limited and is certainly helpless.' Ratnakar stood his ground.

'Now, again you're underestimating the Congress by saying it's helpless in the present situation.' It was Chalpati who intervened now. 'In every area the Congress has its satraps ready to do its bidding the night before the election. The pre-election-night-strategy for them, take it from me, is to reach bottles of liquor, blankets, dhotis and saris, and cash instead of voters' slips to voters and to numerous clubs about whose existence you may not even be aware of. This may put them to auto-destruct mode. But this is the face of the reality.'

Despite the discouraging debate which continued for more than an hour Ratnakar was confirmed his Party had nothing to lose in this election but everything to win.

The second round of tea was ordered because the earlier round's tea for participants in the debate had grown cold in the heat of their argument. Argument and appetite do not go together. It was time, Ratnakar thought, he brought 'paans' for some of those who were deep into chewing them. In fact they were expecting someone to do this service because they couldn't go on listening or even talking for long without betels; and this 'someone' was customarily a younger man of this mob. Though he was younger than many others there, his joining the college had materially altered the relationship. Ratnakar had begun to be treated as their equal, intellectually speaking. Even so he saw no reason for not getting up and go to buy betels for them.

The stars up in the sky looked splendid and the breeze blowing mild was cool. There were other parties—of threes and fours—dotted on the ground enveloped in the darkness. He had to wade through them to reach the betel stall. Suddenly a wave of country liquor's smell struck his nostrils which indicated it was past 8 pm which for non-drinkers was signal to leave the ground.

'Here's this for you.'Madhav said as soon as Ratnakar finished handing over the betels among the group.

'What is . . . ?' He was a little surprised.

'Man and Superman.'

'Oh, thank you. You know Chalpati gave a complete lecture on it the other day when we were returning after seeing a performance of Bernard Shaw's "Arms and the Man" by English medium Southside Girls' High School.' Ratnakar continued.'I was since then interested in this drama because he spoke highly of it. Perhaps now I'd understand what he referred to as Shaw's postulate of "life force."

'That's why I brought this book.' Madhav said.'In fact, I've been carrying this book daily to this place for the last whole week but you were not to be found. I'd almost decided to return the drama to North Institute library if I didn't find you today.'

'Oh, Madhav,don't think of doing that, please, ever.' Ratnakar said. 'I can't help being irregular till election but read this drama I will, I assure you, in a week's time.'

'Bravo!'Chalpati intervened 'And how do you think you'd achieve this marvel? You've exam to face, you've the election to fight, and to compound it all, you say now you'll finish reading Man and Superman in a week! Don't create a chaos of contradictions. Unless you want to end up in a madhouse. Man and Superman needs to be read slowly, in slices, even though you might be doing it in a lighter vein.'

'But he can always read the drama for the second time later if it's that serious.' Mani came to his rescue. 'I believe he can be trusted to perform all three things together.'

The others of the motley group who looked at the academic battle of wits very much wanted it to come to an end so that they could talk about something ordinary like what was cooking in a private Hindi high school committee, like an irregular appointment of a lady teacher in another school. Like.

In the meanwhile Madhav got up.' It's 9 pm and I must be going. On my way I'll ask Papa Rao to send tea for you all. Good night.

'Good night.' Awasthi said, relieved.

'Good night.' Ranga and others joined in chorus.

Nobody minded as Ratnakar stood up to join Madhav since his session was also over.

CHAPTER THIRTEEN

Daughters of a doctor at New Settlement sector, Minati Mohanti and Pragya Mohanti, were twins but strikingly different in some ways in appearance. They weren't fair in looks but could give any fair girl a run for her money in the department of grace. While Minati's specs on her chiselled small nose was an object of magnetic attraction, Pragya's ever-sticking smile on her lips could make her girl friends justly jealous. Indeed they gave the impression of the newly sculpted figures of the same rock that were carelessly set up in this college.

Their slimness accentuating their stature, they were cautiously stepping into Pulin da's cabin which they declared a couple of times was a prohibited zone for them as their parents gave them strict orders not to get into any eatery outside the college campus. In obedience to their parents' wishes they never entered the precincts of this establishment before this moment to his knowledge.

Ratnakar was therefore watching their movement with a little bit of curiosity which though did not last long as they came direct to his table. But belying his expectation that they'd sit down on the empty bench they stood like statues for a considerable moment. Minati broke the uneasy silence saying,'We've something to tell you, Ratnakar 'da,about a matter.'

'Well. Tell me.'Ratnakar gestured for them to sit down.

'Not here. Please come to the college. It's an issue that can't be discussed here.'

'But then what made you come here right now. I'm available in the Union office from 3 pm onward to 5 pm, and you know it. This is just 2 pm. You could have waited for me right in the college which could have saved you the trouble of your coming and being seen in this cabin and . . . . 'Ratnakar checked himself as he realized he was touching a territory he shouldn't.

Minati reasoned,' Our classes were over an hour before the scheduled time. We want to talk about the matter before it's time for us to go. It may be too late if it's postponed now.'

Ratnakar grasped if the issue was not urgent they couldn't have dared to break their parents' edict.

He got up and without further ado started walking straight to the college, accompanied by them, one on each side, like a prisoner, in silence.

'Got any idea which place will suit you for discussion of the matter which you think is serious?' Ratnakar asked her politely, when they entered the campus.

'There,' she pointed to a tree near what was euphemistically called swimming pool.

'Under the shade of the tree.'

They sat on the soft green grass.

'Now, come out with the mystery.'Ratnakar said his harshness vanishing in the coolness of the atmosphere.

'There's no mystery as you say it.' This was Pragya speaking.'The simple fact is that we are pestered by a boy who's getting bolder every day.'

'Minati isn't exactly an ordinary girl. She's a class representative. 'Turning to Minati he said,' Why don't you report the matter to the Principal? He's the right person to stop the boy from troubling you.'

'That's precisely what we don't want.'Pragya replied sharply. 'We don't want the issue to go public.'

'Then what do you want?' Ratnakar was reduced to confusion.

'We want the boy to cease harassing us immediately on our way home. But we want this to be achieved in a discreet manner without anybody getting wise of it.'Pragya expressed her ideas in a well thought-out manner.'We came to you and didn't take the easy option of reporting the matter to the Principal because we're interested in a cautious solution to the problem.'

'It's a tall order, if there ever was one.'Ratnakar was still far from understanding them.' What you want was possible in Middle Ages myths or in some Arabian night's stories.'

'You're making light of the matter because you've failed to appreciate the fact that we come from an extremely conservative family. My father, as you know, is a doctor but he wouldn't take a second to decide to send us packing to our maternal uncle's place if he's to be confronted with an affair or scandal like this. It's not our blamelessness that'd matter to him but the fact of a happening involving his daughters that might put him in what he might consider an intolerable shameful position.' Minati said raising her specs a bit in a serious tone.

'If you've any plan in this regard,' he said thoughtfully,' tell me about that and I'll execute it in the manner you want.'

'If we'd any plan for it why should we come to you?'Pragya was getting irritated 'We're up against a blank. Find a solution or we stop coming to the college altogether. We can't describe it in words but the boy has become a menace.'

'What's his name?' Ratnakar came to the point.

'He said his name's Gopi Chand. What we know is that he's a third year science student.'Pragya replied.

'We shall be leaving in half an hour.'Minati began to say after sensing some relief.'Today is Saturday. You've Sunday. Monday we're not coming. So you have two whole days to think a way out to stop him from harming us. '

'We want to be doctors. Next year we shall be passing out I.Sc. and leaving this college for ever to join some medical college.' Pragya explained the situation sadly 'If an unforeseen storm blows in our ambition's way our career will end up in ruin or worse.'

Minati stood up. If she'd delayed even for a moment Pragya could not have stopped her tears. Ratnakar remained glued to the spot for sometime, after they had gone, trying to disentangle the cobwebs of what he'd heard just now. He was in the habit of thinking on straight lines. For miles he couldn't see any straight line in the conundrum left by these two denizens of a different planet. He could easily leave them to their fate and walk out of this tangle. For a person of Ratnakar's mental make-up who thought of revolution where private dreams and ambitions are banished, these girls' affairs sounded not only meaningless but irrelevant to his main scheme.

But acting quite contrary to his thought processes, he started hunting for Jayanta Naha because it struck him that if there was any solution to the girls' like, he alone could find it. As luck would have it he found Jayanta near the library on the first floor. He was a rara avis for the last two months after a Union's function.

When he laid bare the problem to Jayanta, he made a move to teachers' common room and started ferreting out all three registers of third year science for Gopi Chand's name. He repeated this exercise. The name could not be located as it wasn't there. When Ratnakar thought he was only minutes from solution he found the enquiry blocked at the very first step.

'No progress.' Ratnakar commented sadly.

'I wouldn't say that.'Jayanta said,' The enquiry proves he is a liar too.'

'Is this progress?'

Jayanta did not reply.

When they were returning Ratnakar said to Jayanta, 'I've one more contact at New Settlement. Let me see if he's still in the class.' Since Ratnakar had time only up to Monday he was trying to squeeze things a bit. If he could finish the college part of the mission right today he might hope to be ready with a remedy Monday.

'Well, Sudhir.' Ratnakar accosted him when he was coming out of the class and took him to a corner.'I want to know something about the twin girls. I mean Minati and Pragya.'

'But you must be knowing about them. Minati is with you in the Union. Anyway, what's it you want to know?'

'Have you noticed anything unusual regarding them on their way to New Settlement from the college?'

'Nothing. But of course I saw from a distance a boy following them a couple of times.'Sudhir replied.

'Do you know the boy?'

"Actually I never had any contact with him personally but I came to know about him when he became notorious after breaking a player's leg with his hockey stick in a field. His name is Jadunath Prasad. He's a commerce student.'He moved away as he had nothing more to offer.

It was immense progress for the day, Naha commented after joint stock-taking. He then disappeared in the office but returned in ten minutes. 'Come to my place on Monday. We shall come to the college together.' He said,' And now let's move to catch the bus.'

Wednesday Ratnakar was sitting under the shade of the same tree near the pool expecting Minati and Pragya to turn up with news on their problem. In fact they did not take long to appear there which indicated they were not less interested in reporting the Tuesday's event.

'The boy was not to be seen on our way back home. We stopped our cycles a couple of times to look back to be sure. No. He was not stalking.' Minati said.

'But what if he restarts the mischief today or tomorrow or any other day?'Pragya expressed her doubt and fear.

'Tell me tomorrow if he resurfaces today. I hope he won't, ever.' They departed in a relieved frame of mind after hearing his articulation of assurance.

Ratnakar himself was wondering as to how Naha achieved the objective of getting Jadunath out of the way in so short a time. What Naha told him was that Jadunath had already applied to Principal for Transfer Certificate a week ago and was just waiting for it to be handed over to him. Perhaps he wanted to disappear after committing some kind of crime leaving no trace as wrong identity could only misguide. It was the twin sisters' instinct that warned them of greater danger lurking in Jadunath's conduct on the street that sent them to Ratnakar.

After a fortnight the Mohanti sisters, looking carefree and pleasant walked up to him near the rendezvous. Minati was full of mirth as she handed him a piece of expensive imported chocolate. Pragya asked him with a little playfulness,' Are you a rogue too, Ratnakar 'da?'

CHAPTER FOURTEEN

While most Party comrades and supporters were certain that Com. Harinarayan Mishra would win the election, there was a small section of thinking comrades who did not conceal their reservation about its outcome despite a visible wave of support for their Party as they were also aware of their transparent weaknesses in not being able to provide polling agents inside a large number of booths. What happened in those booths could only be guessed. So ran their argument. But when the result of Kadampur assembly constituency was declared, it was called expected and not surprising: Harinarayan Mishra defeated his nearest Congress rival by an impressive margin.

Even though it was an election victory its impact sent the moneyed class representing varied interests swooning as they could not visualize a situation in which Congress could be humbled in this dusty town. It was the fear of red flag dominating all aspects of Kadampur's life that psychologically unnerved them. But the vested interests soon came out of this temporary paralysis and life returned to normal. Mill and factory owners, big businessmen, moneylenders et al came back to their old tricks of exploitation because the Congress was back in the driver's seat in the State which meant the Government was there to see they continued to do what they had been doing unhindered. But the trade union movement certainly got a boost in the aftermath of this victory. The tremor caused by this movement made local capitalists come to negotiating table several times which was not the case earlier.

Sections of working class and the poor started believing that CPI was a Party which could stand by them in their hour of need. It might sound unusual but the fact was that rickshaw pullers came to the Party office on their own in groups to urge the comrades to form their union to resist their exploitation at the hands of *** rickshaw khatal wallahs ~ rickshaw owners ~ who gave rickshaws to pullers on hire, and municipal staff and police, not to speak of powerful people who gave them less fare than what was agreed to. The problem of rickshaw stand gnawed at them.

Harinarayan Mishra intervened personally in quite a few cases of dispute between rickshaw pullers and passengers right on the spots and made the mighty or dignified passengers pay them their legitimate fare. The defence of rickshaw pullers in this absolute manner shot up Com Mishra's image among them. To cut a long story short, he became a visible face or force at most rickshaw stands. They got an identity, they thought, because of Com. Mishra. They became persons.

With the victory magnifying the Party morale, organizational activities at several levels increased manifold. It was then that the union at a chemical extract factory where about 400 people worked drew searching attention of most Party men because of problems created by the railway by not supplying the required number of wagons to the owner to bring raw materials and send finished products. Under an old arrangement the railway made tracks which passed across a municipal road to reach inside this factory. One coal-powered engine used to carry wagons for unloading-loading goods purposes. The railway administration's decision to give fewer number of wagons than asked for and to delay their supply could not but be described as arbitrary and whimsical. That this whim had put the factory owner at a great disadvantage and loss was no concern of the railway. But if the factory existed, so did the workers. The workers' union had, on the one hand, to fight against the management's exploitation, and on the other, help it get required number of wagons from the railway. Clearly,Harinarayan Mishra's turning a member of the legislative assembly (MLA) increased his clout in official circles of railway but it still fell short of the necessary force to get results. The union had to learn to strike a balance between being friendly and hostile to the management. A trade union could not continue without being constructive in the present set-up.

Com.Santra, who was a worker himself, was the secretary of this union. He had a hard time disciplining the workers and explaining them union's limitations.

Who said the Party had no dreamers? Kadampur Party had one in Shanti 'da. After delivering papers to subscribers or selling literature he would come back to the Party office and sit at a place keeping distance from other comrades losing himself in thoughts. Asked by friends he'd reply he was witnessing a big red flag, almost sky-size, being unfurled at Red Fort. He'd insist he saw this happening from a close range. He said he was thinking about that.

Shanti da might be laughed at as a foolish dreamer or dismissed as a psychiatric case. But what about those who saw the same dream but did not talk about it? To say Kadampur had not its quota of dreamers would be utterly unrealistic.

In the Party office Durgapada Ghosh was thinking loudly about the provision of co-option of an outsider as a member in the chemical factory union. He was told by Com. Santra, the union's secretary, in a recent meeting that a member from the Party could be immensely helpful in the union at this moment for strategic reasons.

Biren Chakrabarty looking at Durgapada slowly said, choosing every word, 'Ratnakar can be co-opted as a member in the workers' union.'

'He's busy preparing for his final examination right now. Think of some other name. For instance, Jagadish Rao.' Naveen Mitra was not in favour of Ratnakar's name because he was doing a good job as a student leader, and disturbing him wasn't likely to bring any luck to the workers' union which was currently going through a bad time.

'But he fits the bill.' Durgapada insisted.

'Then ask him. He might consider it after his exam. His opinion is necessary if he's sent to the union as a co-opted member' Mitra argued.

'I think it's not a simple matter.' Biren da smiled. 'Since the issue of co-option has to be discussed in any case in the Party meeting, we have to wait as other suggestions are also likely especially from Mishra da.'

When friends in the Party office were discussing whether or not to initiate Ratnakar into trade unionism he was scratching his head over publication of college magazine the articles for which had already been collected and were lying with him without any further processing. Though elected secretary of literary and magazine section, Ratnakar had one shortcoming: He was not as proficient in Bengali as in Hindi and English. Except for a few write-ups in Hindi and English all the others were in Bengali which sent tremors down his spine. In addition to selection and editing, the process of publication of the magazine,he thought, involved finding a printer or publisher,reading proofs, keeping time schedule and a lot of other things. The problem,to him, was intractable. Ratnakar became acutely aware that he alone could not complete the job in the expected manner and time. It was then that the name of Alok Sarkar, who preceded him as secretary in the same section, struck him with a force. He had passed the IA exam the previous year and was still to settle for a college in Calcutta for further studies. This youngman had already come to limelight for having published a book of poems in his school days. Since he was far ahead of others in knowledge of publication matter, Ratnakar considered, he could be approached to seek his advice, as he had not left Kadampur yet. But would he help him in publication of magazine which involved both time and physical movement was the question that stumped him. It was quite true Alok was not a stranger to him as Ratnakar had occasions to meet him before he joined this college. Ratnakar tried. He discussed the problem with him and sought his opinion about it all. Alok went much further than expected and told Ratnakar he was prepared to take full responsibility of magazine's publication if he did what he was expected to do in the union's meeting. Which of course was routine. The effect of this friendly and generous act was that he was relieved of a mental pressure which was increasingly becoming intolerable;

and was free to engage in other organizational activities. Thankful? No. Because he remained ignorant of the art and science of publication for ever. But of this, some other time.

Ratnakar's Victoria ground * adda friends were not devoid of talents If Chalpati was a scholar of English of note,Mani—though a graduate of science—was an excellent speaker of English in his own right. What contributed to his commendable faculty in speech was the factor of his dwelling in Southside, an enclave of railway officers who, even after the departure of the British officers, kept the flag of English conversation up exclusively in this area. His father's being a railway officer had naturally something to do with this facility in the language. But unlike his father, he cut for himself a non-railway career of a teacher in a private high school. And because he preferred this profession to a job in the railway he was cut-off from the mainstream of railway's way of life. He turned a casual visitor to this * adda.

But Mani had one more talent: he was a story writer on short notice. Give him a pack of Charminar cigarettes and two hours and, it was said, you'd get a well-written short story in return. Just like that.

Since Ratnakar had enough space in the soon-to-be-published college magazine for Hindi articles, even after absorbing the ones he had, he requested Mani, an outsider no doubt, to write a short story in the magazine. The short story captioned *** Kammo was ready the next day. It was a love-story slightly departing from the ordinary run of stories of the day. It was published in some student's name. The magazine was in the hands of the students in time, courtesy Alok Sarkar.

CHAPTER FIFTEEN

Ratnakar, after his exams were over, became detached and cold about the result in the manner of a Hindu follower of the Gita ~ do your duty and don't wait for the consequences ~ because he took a chance merely to have a go at them. Facing exam was, he liked to think, a kind of duty, and having performed it, he earned the right to immerse himself in Party activities. Whether it was Party fund collection at the workshop gate or at any other market place he was ubiquitous with other comrades urging, persuading people to donate in the paper-covered handy tin boxes. They also had coupons on occasions such as collection for flood victims, or sufferers of other natural calamities in any part of the country. Encouragingly, the Party's stature was growing in the minds of the people the evidence of which could be found in sale of socialist Soviet publications and Marxist literature. This at least established that a section of Kadampur people were genuinely interested in the slogan-shouting anti-Government communists. Ratnakar began to keep a diary for the programme of participation in processions of students, workers or Party men at different points of town on different dates. Previously he relied on memory for his part of the work and didn't have to worry much on this count. The truth was he was made to maintain it because if he had to take part in the increasing load of work and not turn himself a butt of criticism or jibes for his failure in programme because of forgetfulness or negligence, diary was indispensable.

Nobody turned a communist sympathizer, not to speak a member, out of his volition suddenly. For making a man its sympathizer, the Party had to give hours and weeks first to allay his suspicions; and then persuade him to see that it could be a useful weapon in his life's struggle. But the wheel of Kadampur had begun to move in the right direction. Ratnakar had soaked enough knowledge and experience to feel that this was the career cut for him like some other whole-time comrades.

When he was in this state of mind the news came that he passed the IA examination in first division which surprised many, given his busy schedule in recent election. Nothing could bring him more jubilation than this astonishing result. But would it change anything in terms of his career ? He couldn't suppress his elation at the result as it opened other doors for him. The Cassandras who predicted those who worked for the Party or the union election ~ students should not take part in politics brigade's song ~ could not perform well in the examination stood belied.

Ratnakar had become so much part of the Party organization that it was almost unthinkable that he would leave it to seek admission in any Calcutta college for further studies. If he had, after all, to do whole-time Party work, some comrades persuaded him in all their sincerity, what difference would it make whether he studied in Calcutta or Kadampur. Ratnakar was of course free to take his own decision but there was something called moral pressure and emotional bonding in the environment which ultimately won the day. He joined BA class in the same college from which he passed the previous exam.

Ratnakar was cycling his way to Victoria ground to enquire whether Madhav had brought the two books he asked him to. When he was taking a turn he came across a face in the crowd that looked familiar but he couldn't immediately locate her. As she was walking on foot she passed by him slowly with a recognition on her face which broadened into a matronly smile. Wasn't this the woman with whom Jagadish Rao and he worked together in the vaccination drive when Kadampur was reeling under the impact of smallpox? Pretty much, his mind answered. There used to be one more elderly woman with her—a widow in white sari. They were municipality appointed health workers of some sort with all the paraphernalia of cotton and liquid medicine and the injection or something resembling a small pencil with circular teeth. And they were asked by the Party to help these ladies in their work of inoculation against smallpox in different localities. They were then school students though. When the smallpox was taking an epidemic form, the Party couldn't remain a mere idle spectator. It must be by the side of the suffering people. Since the health workers were very few in number ~ that too was as a result of CPI's strident demand ~ it came forward to help them. For the two health workers or vaccinators the area was too wide to cover. Jagadish and Ratnakar, overcoming their initial hesitation in accompanying the ladies, worked with them and learnt a lot themselves about the necessity of this * tika (vaccination) programme. They spoke to all the members in a family if any one of them was suffering from this disease. The idea behind vaccination was to prevent it. It was a big task for them~ arguing against their misconception about the disease, dispelling their superstition in the fifties. It was only when the medicine was finished that they stopped work for the day. A couple of such health workers were clearly less than inadequate for the localities allotted to them. And that's where they came in. They also did the same thing under their instruction.

Jagadish Rao and Ratnakar joined this mission out of a profound sense of idealism but some others tried to put a different construction on this joint work doubting their motive. Was their act inspired by just some missionary spirit? They asked. Or, there was more to it? That they were too elderly for the boys was no stopper for the story tellers.

But the woman who he saw just now passing by him had undergone a striking change since they worked together in the campaign: vermilion on her forehead was missing and she wore a white sari as her colleague did in the past. It pained him to note that she also became a widow. Even when her husband was alive life was difficult for this woman from lower middle class. Why else would she come out to do a job for a pittance of salary? How much more arduous would be life when her husband was no more?

He had read enough to understand that Soviet society had overcome all these problems of hunger, housing, employment. Women were equal to men in every sense of the term and hospital facilities were free. Everyone got according to their abilities. And it wasn't a dream; it was a reality. But this kind of society did not come out of evolution but revolution. And revolution needs as precondition coming together of historical forces for it to happen.

Ratnakar was nearing Victoria ground. He spotted his set.

'Congrats.' Chalpati said joyously.

'You really surprised us.' Madhav said making room for him to sit on the ground.

Ratnakar felt overwhelmed that his *adda friends were so interested in his exam result. When they returned to what they were doing ~ discussing setting up a cultural organization where they could do something creative, Ratnakar put his concept of a library as an alternative to this *adda.

'You've your library but we must have this *adda. Nothing at the expense of Victoria ground's green grass '. Ranga was quite serious when he spoke thus.

'But whoever suggested that this *adda would disappear if the proposed organization takes a shape.' Ratnakar tried to clarify his idea.'For instance, during rainy season, when we can't continue assembly here, we can go there to talk. We can surely return to Victoria ground when the rain stops, can't we? Long live Victoria ground.' At this all of them laughed.

Since Chalpati was interested in bringing all the others round to his point of view, he said choosing his words,' You see, this *adda has to be kept in tact. Agreed. But you can't belittle or ignore the necessity of a cultural set-up to have an identity in the society we move. And what's wrong if we try to find it?' When he found all of them were interested in the idea he was pursuing he continued.'in the evenings some of us do private tuition for a living, and others follow other vocations. And yet our meeting continues. In the same manner, if we set up a cultural centre it won't affect green grass *adda while the centre will continue on its own steam. I don't see any contradiction between the two."

Though nobody argued against Chalpati, pleased some of them the idea did not, Ranga being one for what was in danger was the chance of drinking a glass of white country liquor in great company. It was the feeling of being left severely alone to drink the liquor that caused his frustration and pain, and rebellion.

Ratnakar asked Madhav,'Where are the books you promised to give me?'

'What books? Let me also see them.' It was the voice of Sir Indersingh of Daich who kept silence through out the previous proceedings.

Ratnakar did not know how this short man of about 35 with a wealth of flesh from neck downward came to be called Sir Indersingh of Daich but he was recognized by this name in this crowd. He was reputed for kicking one job after another and getting the work he sought without having to produce a certificate of experience at any interview. He must have had some mysterious resources not known to others that landed him in jobs as varied as school teaching and keeping accounts. He booted a job in Calcutta and knocked one in Kadampur and became Sir Indersingh of Daich in this company. They all liked him for his gentle behavior.

'They're English books. Actually French novels translated into English.'Madhav said this to deter him.

'Let me see the books.'Daich repeated his plea.

'All right. So you will.' Madhav said." Mind it they're English books.

'But I know English too.' Daich persisted.

Madhav went to his cycle, found the two books, and threw them in front of him.

'Abey, it's Hindi.Nana ~ maternal grandfather, isn't it?' Daich said.

'Read what the other book's title is.'

'Madam Bobharai.' Sir Indersingh of Daich read.

Chalpati and Mani felt uncomfortable.

'That's all, Madhav. Finish it here.' Mani said.

CHAPTER SIXTEEN

Ratnakar became aware of the importance of the chair he was occupying in the Party office, albeit temporarily, with others on the two sides of the benches, when a middle-aged man entered and started narrating his experience of torture in provincial 36-garh accent at the hands of one Sattan Maharaj who forced him to sign a sale deed of his small landed property with a dwelling in it where he lived with his family. It took all of them some time to decipher his incoherent phrases which he blabbered out under stress of fear and loss. The matter became clear only after repeated questions were put to him at each juncture. Another dimension was added to his present state of mind: He was now terrified that Sattan Maharaj would surely kill him for coming to the CPI office and reporting the transaction.

Clearly, the matter was such that they couldn't take prompt action. It was an issue that needed Party's deliberation. Only senior leaders could take spot decisions. Actually, for quite some days the tales of Sattan Maharaj's forcible collection of interest from small, gullible borrowers were pouring in the Party office. In some cases, even where full repayment had been made by the borrowers, injustice was done to them, taking advantage of their defenselessness. The Maharaj had a shining *tilak on his forehead and a *Mirjapuri lathi in his hand, and two body guards when he moved in his locality, or even outside. Most people on both sides of the street would be heard respectfully saluting him *Pranam Maharaj or *Palagi Maharaj. Nobody could guess from his saffron gown of a religious person that a cruel Satan existed behind or in it.

The threatened narrator was asked to wait for Harinarayan Mishra who was expected to come any moment. Mishra flew into a rage as soon as he finished the harrowing tale of his loss of property, and asked the comrades to collect some people for a showdown with the perpetrator of the torture machine which could no longer be avoided. He rang up a few contacts and asked them to rush to trade union offices to organize sending emergency help to Party office.

The victim, whose name was Itwari, was sweating, his throat gone dry. But he did manage to say,'Babu, you don't know how dangerous a man is he. I saw him beating some people barbarously and left them only when he thought they were dead. He has quite a few men to do his bidding. Nobody dares speak against him in the locality. You see, none came to my rescue in the whole area when he forced me to sign in public on the sale deed of my house.'

'We shall try to get you back the deed document.' Com. Mishra said in a calm voice.'These men are ready to go with you to his house. You just identify his house.'

'No. I can't go with them.'Itwari looked mortally afraid.

'All right, you stay here in the Party office, then. But give us his accurate address so that they can find him easily without asking others there.'

He gave the address as perfectly as possible, and said: 'There's a temple near his house which nobody can miss.'

The number of people assembled in front of the Party office exceeded fifty which was considered enough for a confrontation if it came to that. Since there was a comrade among them who knew all about what Itwari talked, he led the way to the notorious moneylender's house. By the time they reached the spot Sattan Maharaj had fled his house and gone into hiding. The news of workers gathering near the Party office together with Itwari's presence there was sufficiently alarming for him to put two and two together and give the slip.

It was a march to no result. The workers came back empty-handed.

Com. Mishra phoned town police station. Accidentally, the inspector of p.s., known as *Bada Babu, was available at the first ring. He asked him to register a diary of banging and torture of the victim who, he said, would be accompanied by one of his Party men. He requested him to investigate the case and take action.

Turning to Itwari he said,'Itwari, be a brave man and go to police station.'

'But . . . 'Itwari hadn't even the courage to defend his property.

'No but.' Com Mishra lowered his pitch and said in a persuasive tongue,' That young man'd go with you.' The man pointed was Jagadish Rao.

When they left for police station, Ratnakar asked Com. Mishra :'Do you think police would take any action in this matter ?'

'Perhaps not much.' Mishra said.' Perhaps not at all.'

'Then why this diary?'

'Because this is reporting an illegal action.'Mishra said.' We're not leaving it at just that. We've to complete the job we started today. We've to corner him in a week's time. And this time he won't be able to escape.'

CHAPTER SEVENTEEN

S ince Ratnakar was also a part of the squad hunting the notorious moneylender his memory got refreshed when they were passing by the back of a school where a momentous incident took place some years ago and where he had to lead processions of students quite a few times. A fiery and emotional Hindi speaker was how some estimated him. But, he realized later, he was neither fiery nor emotional. The incident that occasioned these attributes to him was the dismissal of a teacher which created a row that was never witnessed in the school's history and in which he led students' movement in favor of the teacher.

N.S.Balanandan, Nandan to his friends, worked as an assistant teacher in this Hindi high school. Born in a Brahmin family and brought up in Anglo-Indian ambience, he had enough reasons to feel different from, if not superior to, others in the school. Instead he came to be known as an astonishingly generous and mild-mannered man who never let his colleagues feel that he was not one of them. With his disarming free culture he mixed with the staff and became popular with them. Since he was basically a devoted teacher he became an instant success with students.

But all was not well with the school. Though it was affiliated to the State's high school board, it was a private school. This created all the problems. Its managing committee, by which was meant its president, was the last word in all matters. Decisions were arbitrary and consequently the staff lived under unnamed threat. There was of course a way out of this terror. Those who wanted freedom from it had to go to the president's house where he held court much in the manner of a king. The president was a businessman who lived at *Chandani Chowk, a big flourishing railway market at the centre of Kadampur. He never committed the mistake of appointing teachers on the basis of merit, and eased those out who dared to differ with him on any issue. It was a wrong place for Nandan to be in. He never went to his *gaddi to pay respect to him.

The result was he was discharged from service by a one line order not showing even a ground. But this time the president did not reckon with the change in political scene that had already taken place and the teacher's immense popularity among students and his equations with some important people outside the school. The students came out in large numbers to protest against what they considered the unjust act. A strike was organized by students of other schools in sympathy with the striking students of the Hindi school who lay a siege to it demanding the headmaster to bring the president in the school to withdraw his order of dismissal. Though the president tried to influence the town police station, the administration in face of the angry protest, played the justice card. The president had to beat an ignominious retreat.

The withdrawal of dismissal notice was undoubtedly a victory for Nandan who was reinstated in his post with no break in service; it was a pyrrhic victory because he lost in the process quite a few friendships. Majority of the staff sided with the president while the rest were just silent. So, what followed in the school after his reinstatement was an uneasy calm with earlier bonhomie being a thing of history. When people come face to face with the question of eking out an existence the moral principles of friendship or honesty which they otherwise glorify disappear. It is the principle of existence that becomes the supreme guide. The colleagues continued to go to the president's house to dance attendance upon him, while Nandan,in his victory, became isolated and turned a sadder man.

How the president,Bhajanlal,came to wield such enormous power in his person was a wonder to many. He had the inspector of schools verily at his beck and call and, it was said,nothing against the managing committee could ever be officially registered there whoever might be petitioning, complaining against any fault of the school. Mr. Lal rarely, if ever, visited the D.I. of schools office which was situated in the district town ten miles off Kadampur. It was all the way a play of money power, except that all the money belonged to the school. How he siphoned off this money from school must remain a mystery. A couple of teachers handpicked by Lal especially for liaison job at the DI office would do exactly what the president wanted them to do. Obviously, it was this strength of manipulation that made Lal cling to this post and power for nearly 12 years till the present event burst, without ever having to face any election. He surely had the brains to pull strings _ this man.

What was deeply interesting in this drama was a complete absence of any valid reason in the termination order of the president. Nandan was never known as a communist sympathizer in the society dominated entirely by the Congress. Communist Party of India had just started to open its ideological bag on the footpath. He was not connected with anything communistic. On the contrary, he came from a background which abhorred the very sound of communism. Though there were some instances of teachers being singled out for their harassment for communistic leanings, he never fell in that category. And yet . . .

Nandan never considered he was breaking any of the rules by not going to his gaddi. But he was dismissed like so many others prior to him. If some of them were taken back, it was after their complete and abject surrender to him. Nandan's case could have added another proper number to the string but for a factor. It took the turn it did because the blatantly illegal dismissal was published in a Calcutta daily with wide circulation in the town on the front page with the story given full space. It was because of this blitzkrieg of publicity that the students and intellectuals took the cudgels on behalf of Nandan. The journalist who reported small events came into sudden prominence for his sensational scoop. He was none other than Ratnakar.

CHAPTER EIGHTEEN

When Jagadish and Ratnakar were listening to Chalpati's narration of an anecdote extolling the virtues of one Mr. Bajoria so soon after Bhajanlal's anti-teacher deed in which Bajoria's complicity was suspected, and were wondering whether they were getting the message rightly, Sukhlal Sharma, entered the room somewhat despondently.

'Ah, Sukhlal, come, sit here, please.' Chalpati said to him pointing to a place beside him on the mat, with a smile on his face.

When he sat on the mat Chalpati asked,' Is everything all right?'

'I told you about my problem sometime ago and . . .'

'Yes, you apprised me about your predicament. That was a month ago. But you didn't turn up on the appointed day. 'Chalpati's tone was encouraging rather than complaining.

'I couldn't come earlier because I was searching for some papers which were misplaced. Who knew District Inspector of Schools would require theses papers to release my dearness allowance? I was getting my DA so long without these papers." Sukhlal said.

He handed over to Chalpati two small worn out papers saying,' Please write a reply in such English that the

DI of Schools' eyes remain stuck to it and read it twice to understand it.'

'But I'll write it in a style that makes the points clear in just one reading.' Chalpati said this and then explained why.

He started reading the papers. Since the problem was discussed by Sukhlal earlier, Chalpati knew all that was relevant to his case. While writing the draft he asked Sukhlal a question or two. The matter was ready in 20 minutes during which time Jagadish and Ratnakar engaged themselves in translation of a Hindi passage into English. They were there to do exactly that—learn translation.

Sukhlal could not suppress his happiness breaking into a smile when Chalpati handed him back the finished papers in the friendly atmosphere that obtained there. For the same thing he'd to bow to others. Here he was at ease. Because of this difference a lot of Hindi primary school teachers flocked to him and enjoyed his company.

'Thank you, Chalpatijee for this. You can't imagine how distressed and troubled I was for this.'

'Sukhlaljee, now you're embarrassing me. Aren't you our friend?' Sukhlal was touched.

Before Jagadish and Ratnakar entered Chalpati's house they were engaged in an interesting conversation.

'Where was Chalpati when the agitation was taking a shape—a dangerous shape?' Jagadish Rao asked the question, alluding to what happened after Balanandan's summary dismissal.

'He was present in it right from the beginning. Only you didn't know about it because you're busy with, ehem, your studies.' Ratnakar replied. 'But you ought to have known of his involvement in it as you study in the same school where he teaches.'

'You make me feel stupid.' Jagadish said sadly.' But I tell you he never discussed it in the class.'

'That shows his strategy. He talks about these things after school hours.' Ratnakar said.'He called Ramakant Singh,Subba Rao and other students to his place to put in motion protest of students against the unjust act. Though, as you know, I'm a railway school student, I was asked to take a leading role in it.'

'The picture is clear. But one thing remains to be asked.'

'What's that?'

'How did teachers of other schools come into the Hindi school picture?'

"Here again he took the initiative of approaching secretary of a Bengali school's teachers' association to intercede on behalf of the dismissed teacher. Though he didn't set much hope on their support but he got more than what one could expect. All the teachers en bloc came to his school to stand by the victimized teacher.'

Jagadish Rao never smoked, nor ever chewed betels that made lips red. His only concern was studies. He was rarely seen outside roaming after school hours. But after this incident his respect for Chalpati grew, and he started visiting Chalpati's house along with other students. Chalpati became a walking institution. Even when he was visiting a colleague, he was accompanied by, among others, a couple of students. That he was a moving spirit in some of the public causes of this town should go without saying.

Chalpati had many-faceted personality. No surprise his house became a meeting place for a section of people with literary leanings. Some young Hindi poets and story writers found in him enough to admire his scholarship.

After Sukhlal's departure Chalpati got ready for a walk to one of his friends' place. Though they were trudging their way leisurely Ratnakar had a problem with the cycle he was carrying awkwardly. But this sort of inconvenience had become part of group strolling, a habit. When they crossed the railway level crossing at Mandir gate,Chalpati decided to take a turn towards a narrow lane where three couldn't walk together : one had to remain behind. They reached Pardeshi Master's house which was on the ground floor of Kaminibai's building. The cycle was kept locked in front of his house. Chalpati, instead of knocking at Pardeshi Master's house, started ascending the staircase. Ratnakar and Jagadish were following him not knowing where Chalpati was leading. Pardeshi Master, a primary school headmaster by profession, was well-known to them, friendly and generous. But upstairs of the building they never went. They reached the top floor which had only one room, with the open space occupied by a group of children and clothes to dry. A smell of stale food products mixed in the air.

Chalpati knocked on the door. Promptly the door opened and a middle-aged man, somewhat tall, appeared and greeted him. With preliminaries over in Telugu, he started speaking English. It is then Chalpati said to them: 'This is Mr. E Suryanarayana Rao, secretary of E.Railwaymen's union of Kadampur. I wanted to make this meeting a surprise for both you and Mr. Rao. You're too young to understand but note he's a big man in this field-working class in your parlance.'

'You mean he's secretary of the union office that's situated 3 or four blocs off this place?' Ratnakar asked.

'Precisely that, yes.' Chalpati nodded.

"But why should he live here in this small place when he has the union's whole building with many big rooms under his command?' Ratnakar addressed Chalpati, wondering.

'This is not a proper question to ask because he has just come from Gardenreach and is still a newcomer.' Chalpati was feeling uncomfortable at the unexpected question. Mr. E Suryanarayana had understood the question. He answered: 'I live here because I don't want to misuse the office. Using office for any purpose other than what it was meant for may not be considered proper.'

Chalpati talked to Suryanarayana for some more time. He came here especially to find from him if he was at ease in here. No, he was satisfied, relaxed. When they were leaving the place, Mr Rao took out some papers from his old files and gave them to Jagadish Rao saying,'Read the demands of the union and the correspondence on them. They'll apprise you of the real working conditions of railway men which remain largely unknown to people outside the rail because they don't get published, they never come to light.'

'Oh, thank you, Sir.'Jagadish said.'we both will read them.'

Though the visit to Suryanaryana's place was not repeated, Ratnakar had occasion to see him a couple of times near the union office. Earlier, this union office which was on his way to a library where he often went did not arouse in him any curiosity. Now it had become a subject of interest,however,while passing. In the evening, the union office buzzed with activities with office bearers listening to problems, typing letters to proper authorities for redress, and so on.

'I may not be familiar with all problems or troubles of railway men but I surely know about some of them because, as you know, my brother is a rail engine driver.' Jagadish said to Ratnakar when they were walking together after attending a function.

'Well . . .'

'What's the use of knowing or discussing about a problem when you don't have a solution for them?' Jagadish pronounced his opinion.

'The power of solution lies with the authority. The administration has to be forced to wake up.' Jagadish argued.

'In the one type quarter where I live there's not enough space to put 4 cots but seven people live there.'Jagadish stated.' Where shall I study? And where my driver brother will sleep after his 12 plus hours duty? He needs to be fit the next day to drive again.'

'The only way to get out of this hovel's existence is to start an organized fight.' Ratnakar was agitated.

'That's easier said than translated into act. The railway administration will dismiss those who strike. So,' Jagadish said,' it's better to put up with the situation right now till the time's ripe for a strike.'

'And the conclusion is: all will wait for time to ripe.' Ratnakar commented. Needless to say, the wait continued.

CHAPTER NINETEEN

Ratnakar dashed towards Shamim who was absorbed in a tete-a-tete with Surinder Kaur in Pulin da's cabin.

'Well, well,' he gushed, 'where had you been for the last whole month ? After admission you disappeared from the scene completely.'

'Shamim Saab'd been to Chandigarh.'Surinder replied in a humorous vein.

'But Chandigarh's right here.'Ratnakar's face was a mask of all seriousness. Kaur feigned embarrassment.

'No. There's no Chandigarh here. Not an iota of it.' Shamim appeared to turn the direction of the talk in his clipped accent.'Money flows in Chandigarh. There's flood of it if you know how to catch it. It doesn't even drip at Kadampur. If we go by this yardstick, the contrast is glaring.'

'Did you by any chance go there to collect statistics to propound some theory or, as is common, for sight-seeing?' Ratnakar wondered and was interested in finding out what happened to Shamim there. If anything, he looked somewhat changed.

'Let me put it this way.' Shamim continued, 'If you don't mind, Surinder, let me remark that the dress an ordinary college girl wears there must cost four times more than your dress. That's the kind of life they live there.'

'I don't feel inferior to them just because they don
expensive dresses.'Surinder replied with some acerbity.
Both of them had economics as one of their subjects.

'That's consolation.' Shamim was back to his gurgling
voice.'If you're physically present in that ambience before
them you'd realize what I meant by those words.'

'All right. So you've seen the power of money. The
beauty created or added by money.'Ratnakar said,'But it's
not yet clear what's put you off so much. You look more
morose and burdened than ever.'

Shamim thought for a while before making a
reply:'Well, I've seen another scene too. Just a few miles
off Chandigarh. Rows of sheds and factories. And ghettos.
'He appeared to hover between contradictory emotions.

'Shamim, what you need is a hot coffee to change your
mood. That's all I can think of at the moment.'Ratnakar
suggested. Surinder seemed to agree.

When coffee was served for three of them, Ratnakar
said,'Surinder, I don't know what Shamim meant when he
talked of your dress, but I tell you you look fine in it.'

'Is it an attempt to wean me away from him?' Surinder,
when she wanted, could be a supreme actor.

'No.I'm merely making a statement of fact. I haven't
said as yet let Shamim go to hell.'

Shamim smiled. The purpose of the coffee was served.
Shamim and Surinder Kaur were very good friends. The
border closed there. That was the tacit understanding.

Ratnakar became acutely conscious that after their
admission in BA class the groups that patronized Pulin
da's cabin had somewhat thinned and become irregular.

One reason for it was that newcomers had replaced them which was part of normal process. Shamim was absent for a whole month. Rani Chatterjee, the outspoken,studious girl was not to be found anywhere in the college campus. And Shreya appeared to have lost all interest in the canteen in the absence of Rani. And . . .

Those who became irregular in attending classes must have their own reasons but Ratnakar began to feel the pinch of the problem. He had to build the structure of friendship and organization de novo if he'd to prove his existence. With the infusion of first year students at the Intermediate classes the campus was humming with the clucking of boys and subdued giggles of girls as if the river had found a new outlet, a new channel to flow. He felt he was at the bank of this flowing river, alone and unable to organize a significant section of it in his Students' Federation.

Overcoming hesitation and a certain fear of the unknown Ratnakar approached an attractive girl who just separated from the herd, that is, finished talking with friends and turned to move in a different direction. 'Please I'd like you to be a member of our Students' Federation.'

'And what's that?' She was surprised no doubt, but didn't show any sign of escaping.

'It's a students' organization looking after their interests sincerely,' he said.

'Well, I'm in a hurry to catch the bus,' she said looking at him.

'Please take this leaflet. It'll tell you all about us. You can fill up the membership form tomorrow.' Ratnakar was hopeful.

'But I may not come tomorrow.'

'A fresher shouldn't absent herself from the classes in the beginning of the session.'

She didn't make any reply and mingled with her new group of friends. He regretted talking in the tone of a guardian because nobody liked that.

Apparently she wasn't interested in his Students' Organization. Nor even curious about the leaflet which, though, she kept in her bag. But it was her dress material that made him curious and raised in his mind a few questions. It was a simple saree and blouse combination worn commonly by majority of girls. Yet she stood apart from the crowd. Ratnakar had to wait not only for tomorrow but for some more days to know about her.

Ratnakar was sitting under the shade of a neem tree's thick foliage near the swimming pool which appeared deserted even by stray birds at this hour. Between where he was resting and the main building of the college was situated this large tank which made the building look at once near and far. The spot because of this perhaps did not draw much attention of those who strolled to and fro their classes. If he was an object of some attraction in Pulin da's cabin, his existence here was ignored.

It was nearing midday and the college was at the peak of its life. But he remained unaffected by its zest. What drew his lazy eyes was a couple of wild plants with tiny flowers alongside the long grass just a few feet from him. Though he wasn't thinking of anything in particular, his gaze was fixed at them. He was not feeling drowsy despite the mild blowing wind.

A sound of someone's approaching him from behind broke his thread with those tiny flowers of no description. It was the same girl who a few days ago didn't entertain his entreaty to be a member of his Students' Federation, and left him disappointed. No girl struck him the way she did. Could beauty be so stunning ?To be sure he didn't remain the same person he was after his first encounter with the girl. And she was here again right in front of him.

'May I sit here?'She said, a little abashed.

'Please do sit down. It's very generous of you to come to this place.' Ratnakar was controlling his nerves.

'I want to fill up the form of SF membership. And I can't sign it without having to sit, can I?' She appeared to justify her act of sitting. When she made herself comfortable on the ground he asked her: What's your name?'

'You'll soon know it. I'm writing it.'This was Ratnakar's turn to feel red in the face. He ought to have known her name by this time, must be the thought on her mind.

She read the name herself "Chameli Chatterjee" and put her signature at another place.

Ratnakar was looking at her face when she was busy in the act of writing as a school girl. She was perhaps aware of it.

She handed him back the completed membership form saying, 'I'll pay you the fee for it tomorrow. Find me in the common room, please.' She rose.

"By the by, where do you live?'

'If this becomes necessary any day, ask Soma 'di. She replied. A smile flitted across her thin lips.

When she started moving Ratnakar saw some groups of students watching her. The place which not long ago was insignificant temporarily acquired importance.

What was he doing now lying by the pool, leaving Pulin 'da's cabin, absenting himself from classes,abandoning friends, distancing himself from all ? The answer was the face of the enchantress who left minutes ago But if he'd a feeling of love why didn't he find a way to express it when she was here, so close? Prompt came the answer this time: He couldn't communicate it because he didn't know enough Bengali to do it. He was afraid he might stammer or falter. Or just fumble for words. Which might look still clumsier.

It was a reality she came here, sat and signed the membership form. He stopped at this point. If she could sign the form, which was in English, without knowing much English, why couldn't he express his thoughts in Bengali which he knew better than she did English ?Ratnakar now felt not knowing enough Bengali was just an excuse. But where do all these thoughts lead to? The tunnel of darkness. This couldn't go on. He must find the light.

Only a friend could get him out of this mess. His thought immediately turned to Jayanta Naha.

In the meanwhile information filtered that she lived at Srikrishnapur, an area mostly inhabited by refugees from Bengali speaking East Pakistan This was a colony of typically middle class families with a couple of ponds thrown in in the block to give it the right look in the ambience of this town. One could detect from their dialect which part of E.Bengal they came from.

With his obsession growing for Chameli and affecting his work schedule he decided to visit Jayanta Naha. He found him engrossed in Communist party literature. The half-opened books were spread over the table alongside scribbled papers. None of them seemed to be text books.

'Jayanta, you didn't come to college for the last whole week. I can't do justice to the problems of new comers without the organization and you.' Ratnakar said.

'I thought my presence there was not necessary because you didn't come to me. But I waited for you all the same.' Jayanta replied.

'There was a reason for the break in the continuity. For my not coming here. That's one of the reasons I came to you now.' Ratnakar wanted to be candid with him.

'Then tell me what stopped you.'

That I'll. But I'm saving it for the time being. I'll tell you on our way to college in a rickshaw.'

As soon as he narrated his woe and fixation without naming the girl Jayanta interrupted,'Aren't you talking about Chameli ?'

'But how, in the name of God, did you know that? I didn't tell about her to anybody.'

'Well. I won't blame the girl. The blame lies with those who misunderstand her. Since your emotion for her is an extremely personal matter, you and nobody else can decide it.' Jayanta stopped as he didn't want to elaborate further on her. He, however, looked at Ratnakar to find out whether he was taking his statement in the proper spirit. Jayanta knew Ratnakar was a serious person and simple to the extent of taking things on what they appear to be and not what they are.

While descending from the rickshaw near the college Jayanta suddenly burst into a laughter and said,'Whatever you do, remember you're our organization man here at least for two more years. You'll have enough time to straighten things up after that on the other front.'

CHAPTER TWENTY

Some events, when they happen, take on a stranger look than fiction for they are beyond ordinary comprehension. You don't want to believe in them, miracles being a thing of the past. But what if the experience confirms them? Cynicism must take a back seat before the experience. What happened to Sattan Maharaj who was cornered by a CPI mob for taking illegally and forcibly Itwari, a poor man's landed property and who succeeded in somehow escaping from them fell into this category. His heart underwent such change after this event that he not only returned the land deed to the borrower but excused him the whole principal. His good Samaritan act just didn't stop there. In one month's time he got himself rid of money lending business altogether and started sitting in the temple of Hanuman he built earlier in front of his house, depending for living entirely on rent from a couple of rows of houses. He devoted his entire time worshipping Hanumanji, chanting Hanuman Chalisa reportedly from memory. He confided to those who listened to him that he was grateful to Harinarayan Mishra for showing him righteous path, the path of honesty. The news of this change of heart and his sentiment of gratitude for Com. Mishra reached the CPI office too. It could be a feeler of some kind, some surmised. But the majority of comrades were inclined to believe this transformation to be genuine.

'In the coming municipal election he could be made our candidate from his ward. His gratefulness to Mishra da is real. I can vouch for that "said Com Bankelal.

'But before that we've to find out whether he's willing to contest the seat at all. Even if he agrees to, what if he says that he'd do so as an independent candidate.'said Hazra.

'That won't be a problem,' said Mishra da,' we shall cross the bridge when we come to it.' Com Mishra da was not interested in discussing things not in existence. The matter was still in a state of hypothesis.

Whether he actually contested the forthcoming municipal election under their banner became immaterial to the comrades. What was significant was Sattan Mahararaj's desire to associate with the Party and because he was after all an influential person in the locality he could mean quite a lot in terms of votes. In other words, he could be a gain for the Party with his antecedents erased.

The Party had so many things in the fire at the moment. The district committee had fixed a quota of Rs 10,000 for Assam flood victims from Kadampur. Workers of one chemical factory and two beedi factories were already on strike and dharna. Add to this the assembly session which meant that Com. Mishra would himself not be available for most of the time here. Unless full and right kind of propaganda was made inside the railway workshop, the gate collection wouldn't yield much for Assam flood affected people. The immense task taxed organizing abilities of leaders.

Biren Chakrabarty was heard to say,' I'm kept out of the workshop gate collection. Since I'm confined to coordinate activities of beedi workers on dharna I'll do that. At intervals I'll sell Party literature at Chandani Chowk.'

'Are you going right now to Chandani Chowk?'asked Krishnapada.

'Yes.'

'Please take these copies of Swadhinata.' he handed them over to him.

When the Party was in such whirlpool of activities he couldn't stand aloof even if he wished. He,like others, had his quota to complete. He had not only to collect fund from students of the college but also to enlist their cooperation in making student squads to collect public donation at some specific market corners.

'Ratnakar da, I can come to your squad Monday and Wednesday at 10 a.m. That is, two days of your three-day programme. Friday I shall be out.' Rima announced.

'What about you, Ketaki?'

'Well, only on Monday. But it's possible I may give you another date while I join you on Monday. 'Ketaki, the first year student, was hesitating for some reason.

'This isn't a month-long programme.'he said,' we have only one week's time. Assam flood victims need immediate relief. Remember, the chance to do work for others may not always come your way.' Ketaki looked at Ratnakar for a moment, then slowly bent her eyes.

Ratnakar had a list of 8 boys and 2 girls already with him. Rima and Ketaki made it 12 which he thought was sufficient for the purpose. Even if some of them skipped, the programme would stand without being materially affected.

To say Ratnakar didn't think of Chameli Chatterjee once in a while in the midst of action-full of his life would be negating a truth. Actually he'd learnt to live in two worlds. One was the world of ideals to which he remained dedicated despite all the odds. The other world, about whose existence he was unaware till the other day, was for him full of mysterious invitation. When Chameli filled the form under the shadow of the tree sitting close to him she was every inch real. Now she was on the other side of the pool, turning an elf, with the distance growing. He felt he didn't have the wings to fly to the other side where she dwelt among trees and flowers. The elemental force seemed to intervene somewhere.

The reality has the attribute of pinching a man in one form or another if he ignores it for a long time. Chameli Chatterjee, the reality, couldn't be thought of without reference to his family and their social standing and aspirations. But wasn't that jumping too fast ? Perhaps. In that case the relationship that he was visualizing couldn't be one beyond station waiting room acquaintance prism.

It was past midnight and sleep was still eluding him. He was lying in a cot in the open in front of his tin-roofed study with a mosquito-net set on it. High above the net were branches of margosa tree with small dense leaves blocking his view of the moon. He opened the net slightly; enough to place his head out, and was surprised to see the moon as if it had moved to the spot for his benefit. Between his eye and the moon he could perceive hundreds of lines of bright light racing towards him and somewhere in the middle. Were they communicating some message to him? If so, he couldn't decode them. But he fell asleep in that position. When, he didn't know.

He woke up in the morning to a slew of programme lined up for him starting from writing posters in the Party office for a mass-meeting five days hence at Victoria ground, to a students' meeting in the college, to visiting an ailing comrade in the hospital in the evening. In a matter of minutes he finished everything including breakfast and was on his way to the office on his creaking bicycle. He knew the cycle needed repair badly. But where was the time for it?

The office was open but the scene inside the room he was to write posters was daunting : there was a litter of torn papers and some beedi stubs spattered on the mat reminding one of yesterday's work.Biren da alone was there sitting on this mat without any sign of discomfort in his usual posture of a burning beedi in his mouth, and another doused beedi on the tip of his ear, with a newspaper in his hand.

'Why so early?' Biren da was visibly astonished to see Ratnakar at that hour. 'There isn't a comrade for you to talk to. And the room isn't cleaned yet.'

'I've come to write posters. I promised to give at least 20 posters to Bera and Rao today,'Ratnakar said.

'Mad. You're really mad. You could write them at a comfortable hour during the day as the others do. 'Biren da admonished him.

'Because today I shall be busy during the whole college hours.'Ratnakar explained. 'I can't come back leaving the college in the midway to write posters. I must finish them in all cases before I go to college.'

'I was actually going to lock the office as it was time for my cup of tea.' Biren da laughed.'If you're but five minutes late, you'd have found the door shut.' Ratnakar didn't know what to say now that he was still laughing.

'I'm going out for tea. How long do you mean to stay here?' asked Biren da.

'At least for an hour. Maybe half an hour more.'

'I hope to come back by then. But don't leave the office in any case until another comrade comes.' Biren 'da had his responsibility in the matter.

Ratnakar was so long continuing conversation standing. After Biren da's departure he took the broomstick to clean the area on the mat for him to write the posters. He found the colours safely kept at a place.

CHAPTER TWENTY ONE

Ratnakar paddled his way to Victoria ground because he wanted to feel free from Party and studies albeit briefly and give indulgence to his sense of pleasure, the weather having changed so dramatically: It was summer but the air was cool.There was nothing more enticing for him than Victoria's open space that evening. But a surprise, if it could be so called, waited for him there : the ground was singularly empty of his friends. Normally in such situations, he'd turn back his cycle leaving the ground for a different destination, without a second thought. But the site did not deter him this evening because he really wanted to enjoy the weather and the ground. To be alone here wouldn't be any less blissful.

When Ratnakar was ruminating in this manner with his eye fixed on a rare green patch of the parched ground, he heard Madhav shout:" Abe, what are you doing here all alone? Where are Chalpati and Awasthi?"

"I didn't go to Chalpati's house today assuming he'd be here." Ratnakar replied. He was taking time to stand his intractable small cycle.

"Tell me about your college. Do you participate in dramatic activities there?"

"The students' union organized song-dance-fests and debates, but drama never." he said," But why do you ask this question? I'm not clear about what you're driving at in this interrogation. Has it got anything to do with the union or the drama?"

"Drama. Damn your union."

In the meanwhile Chalpati,Ranga and Awasthi also arrived and completed the circle. Ratnakar said to Madhav," You've yet to explain your new-found love for drama."

"It's very simple. A well-known director, N.Upadhyaya is interested in staging a Hindi drama. He has got Suresh Arora, a 32-year young man and two girls of 25 for the drama. He needs one more young man who must have proficiency in eloquence. Dialogue must come distinct. And I think you fit the bill. Am I clear?" Madhav stopped.

"But," Chalpati intervened,"Arora has experience of acting in a couple of dramas, if not more, whereas Ratnakar has none. Well . . . it depends. If he has dramatic talent, the problem won't be insurmountable."

"Well, my position is very straight forward. I'd be too young in the company you just mentioned. A complete novice. And I'm not sure about any latent talent. Madhav, you may count me out of it."

"How can you say you're too young to act? If the role is meant for a young man of 23 or 24, you surely meet the requirement. Before saying no to it you should know all about the drama, the script." Turning to Madhav Chalpati continued," You've confused the issue by telling the wrong half of the matter. It has created mystery where clarity was needed."

"Let me complete it. This is a social drama. So far it was played 100 times in different cities. The book is with me. He should read it in three days' time and then give his opinion."

There was some more discussion in which Mr. Upadhyaya was praised by Madhav as a fine director. Ratnakar had his fill and he stood up with the book thinking this was the end of the matter.

On the third day Madhav rushed to Ratnakar's house before going to his office to inform him that a bungalow which was vacant and under charge of Arora's family was arranged for test and rehearsals temporarily and that he must go there in the evening. And he took the book from him and gave him the number of the bungalow.

Willy-nilly he arrived at the spot without much difficulty wishing the programme postponed on some ground. It appeared his friends were present in strength and the participating acting group was already in motion. As they were engaged in their jobs their voices could be heard once one got inside the compound through the gate. Some of them gestured him to come in.

There were eight cane chairs and a bench and yet the space left was large enough to hold a stage. It was spacious obviously and fit for a whole troupe. One girl was sitting on the bench while the other was standing and talking to a fat middle-aged man who, Ratnakar guessed, could be the director. And he was right as the fat man stood up with agility and gestured the standing girl to follow his facial movement and dialogue. She repeated the six-line dialogue fixing her eye on the door (audience), not even for once looking at the sitting girl, without any prompting.

"Good ", the director said,"except that the drama was missing. This is an occasion for grief for you. You've to express a gesture as if you're wiping tears or show some facial contortions to the audience. But don't be disheartened. We shall re-do it after some time."

The director asked Arora to enact a different scene from the drama and handed over the girl sitting on the bench her part of the script. It was more to judge Arora's performance than the girl's who delivered her lines only to prompt him to act. Arora stood up and sat beside the girl. Looking straight at the girl he spoke his lines slowly but audibly and got the reply. He suddenly stood up and took a step or two towards the audience and delivered deftly his talk in anger. Then Arora took a sudden U-turn and advanced menacingly towards the girl. The director shouted,"Stop."

"Are you ready, Mr. Ratnakar?" The director asked but did not wait for the reply as he stood up and started giving him and the girls direction.

"This is not a bench but a table. Ratnakar and Sarika will be sitting across each other, and you Padma, at that end of the bench." Turning to Ratnakar he said,"Start scene seven as soon as I sit on the chair."

But Ratnakar forgot the very first line from his script and looked blankly at nothing in particular for a moment or two when Madhav in the form of deus ex machina with the book in hand from a distance prompted him.

Back to life. He laughed (which was no part of the script) and carried on."I can't bring you the moon. Nor can I take you there. But I can certainly take you to a 3-star hotel for dinner any day next week."

Padma : "Why not today ? Three Aces is open."

Ratnakar stood up, covered the distance of the table and spoke his lines loudly which were supposed to be humorous, prompted by Madhav.

"Thank you, Mr. Ratnakar. We shall be meeting next week again".

Ratnakar never went to rehearsal again. It was one thing to talk to girl friends in a humorous vein in the college and quite another to speak to girl actors, or whisper to them or come close to them all in expectant broad view of the audience. One couldn't be a performer without talent. He recollected he acted the character of one Dhoti Prasad in a comedy directed by Badrinath,the drill teacher,in his schooldays which was performed on the stage of North Institute. Even though the audience laughed, Badrinath commented he did not heed the prompter and spoke what was not in his script and was also guilty of overacting. He might be right which was one reason which made him doubt his histrionic ability for ever.

Madhav said to him one day,after he missed two rehearsals,"Director Upadhyaya did not get your replacement as yet. You still stand a chance. What's required is brushing up your faculty. Though you stand no comparison with Arora who is miles ahead of you in drama department, but Padma believes you can still make it."

"If I speak my lines I forget emoting. When I start expressing my feelings speech gets detached. I'm aware of this imbalance. If I'm unfit for anything it's drama." Ratnakar replied and felt sorry for not coming up to his expectation. "The voice of Drama seemed to call me, but it was a wrong number", as someone rephrased a saying.

Much later he came to know Upadhyay's drama never came to the point of being staged despite several well-attended rehearsals. In a sense Ratnakar did not lose anything on this score. But this also established drama was beyond his ken. To borrow an idea:" I am not always good and noble. I am the hero of this story, but I have my off moments."

Having said that it must be added this did not prevent him from being a critic of the drama as he had read enough about its techniques, rules and conventions both in Hindi and English.

Just about the time they were hunting fun in drama Awasthi picked up a quarrel with his primary school's managing committee without gauging how powerful the boss of this private school was. The trouble was compounded by his stupidity in writing back a reply without consulting his friends here to the secretary's show cause notice. He fell into a well-laid trap because his rash answer was precisely the thing his boss wanted.

On the day Madhav was persuading Ratnakar to take part in the drama, he felt neglected because his problem was not touched. It was taken up by Chalpati the next day whose house became the centre of a series of meetings with relevant papers on the table in a manner. Unless the district inspector of schools intervened, the managing committee might succeed in doing what it wanted to do. One other course was to seek the help of the guardians who alone could deter the secretary from taking extreme punitive action. But it needed full time organization and house-to-house meeting of guardians to convince them of the autocracy of the secretary and motivating them to have a dialogue with him. It was a Herculean task and Chalpati had to take leave for a few days from his school to be available for all hours till the issue was settled to Awasthi's satisfaction.

CHAPTER TWENTY TWO

Ratnakar was analyzing his experiences with those who differed with him on college election issue or adversaries in the college. Among those who left an impression of certain decency despite political differences was Altaf who came from a family known for their riches and connection with the top brass of the Congress Party. A student of Bachelor of Science when Ratnakar was a first year arts novice, he gave him a table talk on the student union election, and finding him interested, drew a complete picture giving details of nomination papers showing the process. How many points are to be checked before nomination papers are filed so as to eliminate the possibility of rejection was the tenor of his discourse. He rained all this information in a disarmingly frank manner interspersed with laughter in an eatery called Doctor da's cabin at a little distance from Pulin da's cabin. Though Ratnakar was interested in the mystique of election, he did not know what he should do with this knowledge then. But when he was given responsibility of organizing students for election later, and when he rushed to Jayanta Naha he found him making precisely the same draft of nomination paper and other factors as Altaf did.

Altaf was of the opinion, at least it appeared so, that students' union election should be allowed to be held without any political label on the basis of agreed list of candidates so as to avoid bitterness among students. This was supposed to lead to healthy functioning of the union. It remained his pious wish because his own outfit rejected it as the later events proved. All this was now past.

"What are you doing about students' cycle stand?" asked Naren Das, a second year student.

"I met the Principal and impressed him about the immediate necessity of a cycle-stand."Ratnakar replied, "Somehow he's not convinced about its priority. He'd other things on his mind."

"So?'Naren was sarcastic. Shall we continue with the disgusting situation? One day a bell gets missing, another day a valve and . . ."

"The students' union is soon going to start a signature campaign in favor of a cycle-stand and other demands. We shall go to the Principal in a deputation with hundreds of signatures."Ratnakar assured him."And this will be done next week. Unless he feels impressed about the majority demanding cycle-stand, he won't budge an inch from his act.

"But why should we have to demand a cycle-stand in the first place? The college authorities should have made a provision for it themselves because a large number of students come from far-off places on cycle."

"That's what you feel. Principal's perception is different. He's unfeeling to students' problems because he thinks they can be sorted out by students themselves."

A boy who was passively listening to this conversation sitting on a nearby bench in the empty class room suddenly came alive, interjecting, "But how can they? Students can put up their bell-top losses or stolen valve experiences, but what if their cycles get stolen? Their guardians might say: either go on foot or stop going to college altogether. They can't replace a cycle each month."

"That's why the students' union has drawn up a programme of action to address your problems, one by one. First you've to join the signature campaign. The rest will follow."Ratnakar's voice got more confident.

"I'll put my signature any day you ask me to on the demands." The same boy said."But what after that? Will it result into what we want?"

'If the deputation with signatures fails, we shall be left with no alternative but to agitate for our demands in a big way. Posters, class meetings and then strike. "Ratnakar said firmly keeping his excitement in check. He looked at the two students, before getting up, who appeared satisfied.

It was a very intriguing situation for Ratnakar and students' union because, on the one hand, the Principal,when apprised of students' problems,would bring up issues of development, a new building, a swimming pool but without moving an inch in any direction, while, on the other, students would clamour for cycle-stand, adequate drinking water and some other basic facilities. Their dissatisfaction and suffering were growing visibly.

Ratnakar, Surinder Kaur, Shreya Bhowmik and some other office-bearers were sitting in the improvised union office, exchanging notes of their work informally when suddenly a person entered the office and said he wanted to talk about the night-shift of the college. He looked much senior to them but a student all right. When he was requested to sit in a chair vacated for him, he ignored it and continued to speak standing.

"It's 4pm. My class starts at 5.30pm. I came to meet the GS or anybody in his place." he paused," I'm Arun Sen, third year commerce. Problem: we can't continue listening to lectures in the room with snakes creeping under our legs. My friends in the class sent me up to tell you to either remove danger of snakes in the room or shift our class to the main building where there's electricity."

"I understand you've a class-representative in this union. He could raise this problem in the office."Ratnakar was trying to pacify him and put him on the track.

"Our class-representative is sleeping or I wouldn't be here." He was fuming with rage." Our class is held under petromax light in a tin-roofed room where all kinds of insects abound at night. One can put up with a stray dog or goat which roams freely in the room but a snake? The college is asking too much."

"You see, Mr Sen, this is a common problem with night section students."Ratnakar said,"however, we shall raise the issue with the Principal at the earliest opportunity after we've talked with your class representatives."

I knew it was useless to talk to union people. You're good-for-nothing chaps." He rushed out of the room in high dudgeon.

After the commotion of the wave that Arun Sen produced settled down, Shreya commented:"So you . . . we are good-for-nothing chaps."

Could students' union transform tin-roofed rooms into concrete structures, or arrange electricity in them or stop snakes from having their day at night in there? But if it couldn't get some of their nagging problems solved, it was equally worth a thought, what it was there for.

Surinder Kaur said:"Apparently night-section class representatives are not seen to be doing anything for them. That's what has come out of Sen's gush. I'm not speaking of solution of problems but the representatives could pressure the night-section authorities into taking some temporary measures to lessen their fear of crawling snakes."

"Now that the ball has been thrown in our court," Ratnakar said," we should find the General Secretary to discuss what little we could do about it."

Ratnakar was a regular visitor to Jayanta Naha's place at Netajipalli which incidentally fell on his way to college. It was routine. As soon as he emerged out of his house in his white robe—dhoti and Punjabi—a rickshaw puller would rush to him as he became familiar and felt pride in carrying an educated passenger. It'd seem he owned both the rickshaw and the puller. Jayanta in rickshaw and Ratnakar on cycle must have looked a common sight to shopkeepers on either side of Netajipalli's road.

It was the third consecutive day when he was told third time by members of his family that Jayanta was not at home. Even before he could ask them where he was, then, they had begun to quiz him about his whereabouts instead as he was his friend and a Party comrade he might know better. He hadn't got the faintest clue about this new development. Very many weeks ago,he recollected, when he came to him to seek enlightenment on nomination papers,he found him sitting before a table which was spread over with books with open pages and some scribbled papers which gave the look as if he was trying to disentangle a complicated matter. Or search references. But he wasn't sure if this indicated he was passing through a mental trouble. He told Jayanta's younger brother that he would go to the Party office that evening to find out if any of them knew anything about his present location.

The picture was different in the Party office that evening with hushed voices about arrival of Indranath Chatterjee from the Provincial committee who was on a tour of this district. Some tendencies which were not healthy for the Party were observed and he rushed to this district to study and settle personal, local and political differences at the district and local committee levels. Since Ratnakar was still new to the Party, though he was dimly aware of Party programme and organization,he was at sea about its practical ways. Durgapada Ghosh was of course there, but he didn't feel like asking him about Jayanta. Nabeen Mitra was not to be found busy as he was meeting a group of beedi workers. Harinarayan Mishra looked happy,signing and stamping all kinds of papers and copies of certificates, brought to him by Party men and others. Ratnakar was so much perturbed over Jayanta that he felt that he was not somehow fitting in the scene. He left the Party office without talking to anyone.

He needed to think out where he stood in relation to the Party. What he could read so far about it seemed inadequate. Unless there was more light in this labyrinth he would never know why he was working for students' organization which seemed a mechanical job to him without any great cause behind it. Was he doing it for the fun of it or there was some ideal in it ? What was the nature of this ideal? How is it related to the materialistic philosophy?

With this disturbed frame of mind where questions continued to repeat he reached Victoria ground for a breather.

"What's new, Ratnakar? Has something happened?" Madhav asked.

"Well, there's nothing new to speak of."Ratnakar was surprised by the question.

"You look morose. Your face reveals what you want to conceal." Madhav said. All the others _ Chalpati, Mani, Awasthi _who were not interested in this turn of talk looked at him.

"You're imagining things, Madhav, and nothing else."Ratnakar tried to get out of this embarrassing situation.

"Then how's that you've been forgetting to take the matter you gave me to type. You should have taken the typed papers last week. You don't remember about that even today." Madhav got sarcastic.

"Oh, thank you." His smile came back electrifying his mind." I was wondering what you were leading to."

"Well here's something new for you." Chalpati said," Meet Mr.Sarbajeet Singh. He's published his fourth novel in Punjabi."

"Very glad to see you in this ambience." Ratnakar shook hands with the 38-year or so old newcomer who was smartly built with no flab for his age.

'Sarbajeet Singh wishes to celebrate publication of his fourth novel here."Mani added his slow laughter to this announcement.

"You are welcome to it." Sarbajeet Singh said looking at Ratnakar.

"But Madhav and Ratnakar will leave when last course is served."Chalpati clarified.

"But why?" Mr. Singh asked.

"Because the last course arranged is Hitler." Mani put in.

Hitler was code for pure country liquor.

CHAPTER TWENTY THREE

Ratnakar wasn't sure of who mooted the idea of Bengal-Bihar merger—the Centre, Bihar or West Bengal—but whoever's brain wave it might be, this created a political commotion in Dr.Bidhan Chandra Roy's Bengal the like of which it never witnessed before. Since the Congress ruled the Centre and the two States, they considered, this uniformity could crush hurdles. But the people of the two States came out in opposition to this horrible concept across political spectrum in a massive way proving their reckoning wrong.

The CPI at Kadampur was slowly but steadily rising to the challenging occasion. When there was an all-Bengal call for students' strike by Students' Federation against this merger, Ratnakar along with other student leaders jumped into the fray. The strike call was supported by others including a section of Congress at Kadampur.

A group of strikers would go to a school and ask, persuade students in the school to come out, and, after they bolted out of it they would march to other schools. The leaders were at the head of the procession shouting slogans. Since the issue was such that it drew sympathy from school administration which didn't try to put any obstacle in their way.

It was a smooth affair except for railway schools which locked the gates and forbade the students willing to join the strike. By this time the number of students swelled to 500 or even more in the procession. Hearing the tale of students' forcible confinement they got furious at the arrogant authorities and did precisely what was a foregone conclusion in such situations: they tried to break the gate and in the melee that followed hundreds of students tore into the school. It was at one such excited moment that Asutosh Banerjee,a leader, boxed a window pane and got severely injured himself in the process. The splinters of the glass cut up to his hand's bone, leaving him profusely bleeding needing immediate medical care. When he was being taken for medical aid he felt sorry he couldn't stay for some more for the cause. It was this measure of sincerity that affected all.

Ratnakar stopped here. In the process of describing students' role in bigger issues of the day with far-reaching consequences, he narrated this episode in Doctor da's cabin to a mixed group of students.

He continued," The student leader who broke his hand in the railway boy's school is sitting right among you." The listeners were confused about who Ratnakar meant. Their curiosity was whetted. Ratnakar slowly announced with a smile on his lips,"Hold your breath. He's no other than Asutosh Banerjee."What followed was the scene of relieved laughter.

Asutosh was beaming with smiles when he said," But what was your point in making me the centre of focus? I must say I enjoyed your way of presenting it, nevertheless. But such things do happen in a movement of this scale."

"Now you're belittling the incident. It was significant because, for one thing, it brought you into prominence and made you a front-ranking leader of Chhatra Parishad.For another,your brave act did not go in vain."

The students began to disperse.Ratnakar also had a class at that hour. The talk had to be ended there.

Ratnakar got information in the college that Jayanta was back home and resting. It was repetition but the fact was that he was a great help in the management of student affairs and he couldn't do without him for a long period. He wanted to dash to him at the first opportunity. But before that to happen he must get the word confirmed because he didn't want to face any uneasy situation like the one he went through before.

Jayanta wasn't the kind of person to disappear for three or four days from the house and remain untraced just for the fun of it. Unless there were extra-ordinary factors behind it, he wouldn't do it. He must be on the track of something which was yet to be revealed. Like . . .

It was Jayanta first who communicated to him in all seriousness that this Communist Party was not the Communist Party it had been. But he stopped just there. It was a Communist Party without any revolution, he said after a long pause.

'What are you saying?" Ratnakar was bewildered.

He did not want to go further on it, again.

"What made you think so suddenly?'

"You mustn't tell anybody. It is secret. Khrushchev, the first secretary of the Central Committee, placed a secret report on Stalin denouncing his violence that accompanied the revolution. It's still a secret in the international communist fraternity. I've got a copy of the report labeled 'secret' which was placed in the 20th Congress of the CPSU. This is a smuggled copy of Khrushchev's genuine speech."

"Is it a message to the international communist movement?"Asked Ratnakar after some thought.

"It's a veiled message to the communist parties the world over what not to do. But this is still secret. Since this is a secret document it will never be official."Jayanta said and cautioned:"Don't discuss it before anybody till our Party issues any notice about it."

It so happened that the very next day Com.Biren Chakrabarty indirectly alluded to the significance of 20th Congress of CPSU in the presence of Jayanta Naha, Ratnakar and Durgapada Ghosh in the Party office when Com Ghosh eyed him to stop the subject. It appeared to Ratnakar that Ghosh didn't want him to know about it and be co-sharer of this elitist knowledge. Ratnakar was a branch member and they were local committee members, to be sure. If Ghosh was prompted by any other nobler idea in signaling Biren da to stop in the midway, he didn't know. But this also exposed his ignorance about Ratnakar's resourcefulness. Ghosh certainly didn't know that Ratnakar had by this time become a regular subscriber to the Statesman, RK Karanjia's Blitz; Shankar's Weekly and Mainstream in addition to New Age. If there was anything deviating, out-of-the-ordinary or startlingly new in the 20th Congress of CPSU, the capitalist Press wouldn't leave any stone unturned to get at it. Ratnakar in fact knew about Khrushchev's 'de-Stalinization' in that Congress but he doubted its veracity: it could as well be a capitalist plant to confound the world communist movement. It must prove false, he earnestly hoped.

It was a dramatic moment somewhat between Ghosh, Jayanta and Ratnakar with irony popping its head somewhere. Personal perceptions, it needs to be stated, may vary from Party's record on this event.

Did Jayanta's present going missing have anything to do with any discovery of some secret like the one he had made earlier about Khrushchev's secret report on Stalin? He must see him now that he had come back, he decided.

He was all alone sitting in a corner sipping tea in Pulin da's cabin, thinking whether he should go alone to Jayanta's house or take some friend along as a companion. But this chain of thought was disturbed as Malini De appeared as if from nowhere and rushed to his table with three of her girl friends.

"I've been searching for you like anything, Ratnakar da. I searched the whole college for you, But you're here." Malini's tongue had a speed that few could match.

"But what's the matter? Why should you run for me like this? You make me feel important." Ratnakar said while making room for them to sit down.

Malini laughed. The laughter was unrestrained and riveted not a little attention from others.

"Important or not, you're the person needed at this moment. These girls want to enroll themselves as members of SF. They are my friends." She replied, and started exploring something in her bag.

"But I haven't got membership forms with me right now. Tomorrow . . ."

"No tomorrow. I've got the forms ready. No worry, I got them filled up by them "Malini cut him short.

"Then why this hunt for me? I really wonder."

"You've only to deposit these forms and fees at the right place. That's all."

"That I will. Anything more?""

"The reason I'm hurrying is that I'm going to visit some relations in Calcutta right tomorrow for a week."

"Now I see why you were pursuing me with extra energy." Looking at three of her girl friends Ratnakar said with a smile,"I think by now you've understood that Malini is as efficient as anybody else. She doesn't need any certificate from anybody for recognition as a competent organizer of SF. Tell me if I'm wrong."

One of the girls said, "This is what you should know better. What we know is that we've become members of SF because of her."

"That's what I wanted to hear." He said politely.

Malini laughed, but didn't speak anything.

"Well, you all deserve a cup of coffee each for the exercise that you put in to reach me." Ratnakar proposed.

"If you feel so, yes. "The same girl said with no hesitation, without batting an eyelid. He was surprised. This boldness also owed to Malini. Her very presence gave strength and confidence to others.

Ratnakar intended to go to Jayanta's place direct from college and he had planned things that way. But after receiving the new membership forms he thought it'd be better first to hand them over to one who'd take them to district office the next day to deposit them. But this meant he had to go to the Party office to find the right person.

He did meet Naha the next day who looked sad and somewhat careworn. He had been to Calcutta to meet some comrades, he said, to find answers to some of his questions that troubled him. He gave Ratnakar the hint that because he raised some points regarding Party's functioning at the local level which made two leaders uncomfortable and that he was likely to be dropped from membership. Since what he said appeared vague to him, Ratnakar decided to wait for things to crystallize themselves, before he made any move to help him resolve the dilemma.

Chapter Twenty Four

Earlier in the day when Ratnakar was coming to college on his bicycle he felt he was passing through a furnace instead of the road. There was suffocation waiting for him in the class-rooms in the college and the professors looked more like jailors than benign teachers. But in the afternoon clouds began to collect in the western sky and in moments the college went under a thick veil of darkness. A light wind began to blow and men and animals alike felt nature's power to give relief when it suited its mood. But about nature's caprices who could know better than animals!

Ratnakar wanted to get away from the college for a while because the exhilarating breeze outside beckoned him and he didn't want to miss its benediction. He looked at the sky which by this time had taken the shape of a black mountain. He was relishing the walk when the drizzle started. Involuntarily his steps moved to Pulin da's cabin.

With the incoming and outgoing of customers both stopped because of the threatening sky, the joint had few students and Ratnakar had no difficulty sighting a table where he could sit. Since from the entrance only the backs of two girls were visible he could not recognize them but he moved to take a chair facing them. They turned out to be Surinder Kaur and Anita, Surinder engrossed in eating hot pakoda, and Anita sipping tea with no sign of interest though in the act. It appeared for a moment to Ratnakar that Surinder for some reason didn't want to be seen munching pakoda there. Perhaps this explained her choice of facing the wall.

"Where is Shamim?" Ratnakar asked Surinder, changing the position of the chair slightly.

She drank half a glass of water to wash down the pakoda before she answered: "What a question to ask. If your friend plays hide-and-seek even at this age, what can one do? He told me he had an extra copy of the prescribed history book which he would deliver me here. But he disappeared since then as a matter of fact."

"He must have been caught in the rain somewhere on his way to this place."Ratnakar tried to defend his friend.

"You can find any number of reasons for his missing. It's obvious in this blistering rain any attempt to move out carrying a book would be utter stupidity. But that's not the point. He was supposed to be here before I came. I had been waiting for half an hour for him before the rain actually started." Surinder Kaur was a sensitive girl who could not put up with any break of what she considered rule.

Anita suddenly cried:"Shamim has arrived."How she spotted him was confounding. She might have turned back at the dramatic moment, synchronizing his entry.

"I'm sorry, Surinder, for keeping you waiting."Shamim said before sitting on the chair. He wasn't drenched as one would have guessed indicating someone with umbrella must have dropped him here.

"So you should be."She said curtly as she felt his saying "sorry" was functional and not sincere.

"I brought the book I promised. You don't have any reason to be so annoyed about it." Shamim found the book in his bag which he brought particularly for carrying it, and put it on the table.

"No further explanation." Anita said to Shamim to break the uneasy state. "And now, what'd you like to have—pakoda or tea?"Then she turned to Ratnakar:"What about you, Ratnakar da?"

"Both."His answer was brief.

"I owe something to all of you." Shamim laughed and stood up.

"Let me do the ordering." Instead of calling any servant to the table he himself went to the cabin's kitchen.

What they saw after a few minutes was not a little surprising. A servant approached their table with a shining tray and still more flashing pots of coffee,milk, and sugar along with other items and placed it on the table cautiously. This just didn't fit the scene of the small eatery.

"What else?" Ratnakar asked Shamim with a smile in jest.

"Hot pakoda. They've neither fish chop nor mutton cutlet at the moment "replied Shamim.

Anita offered herself to do pouring coffee, milk and adding sugar. When adding sugar to the brew with spoon she was asking everybody how much.

The scene transported Ratnakar back to an incident in the past. He started moving in the by—lanes of his memory when Kadampur was going through a convulsion of railway strike and families of strikers were at the receiving end of the administration's fury,with the State police going amok with their batons. When peace returned a heavy price had already been paid. It was at such time that NK Gopalan, MP, came to this town to study the actual condition of the sprawling workshop and workers so that he could place facts in the Lok Sabha about the recent incident. Clearly this was his official visit arranged in consultation with Railways Ministry and the Chief Mechanical Engineer, the top man of Kadampur Rail, accordingly had prior information of his visit and its purpose.

Com. NK Gopalan was accompanied by Harinarayan Mishra, Ratnakar himself and another comrade when the car reached CME's office inside the workshop at the appointed hour through a separate gate, through which cars could enter, meant for CME's entry.

He didn't remember what enquiries Com. Gopalan made and what facts CME and other officials supplied to him but he recollected a particular scene in the CME's chamber when they were seated around a big table. No other place could be more spick and span for Ratnakar than this office. A uniformed serviceman appeared with a tray with numerous pots and other accompanying items, and started putting them on the table uninterruptedly while the dialogue between Gopalan and CME and Harinarayan Mishra continued. Actually he was too young to comprehend fully the proceeding going on on the table but he could follow some of it on the basis of his experience. But about this, at some other time. When the uniformed servant asked Gopalan politely,"How many sugar cubes, Sir?" Gopalan looked at

the material and then said,"Two."

Never before this had he heard the term 'sugar cube' and known what it meant. The term indicated the "class', a few notches above the middle class 'spoonfuls of sugar'. When he was asked the same question he replied, naturally, two. If the servant had asked him this question first he was sure to have been dumbfounded and embarrassed no end for his ignorance.

So when Anita asked him "How much?"he said "Two" involuntarily. But it was the measure of sugar. Anita was so junior in the company that she could have passed for a school girl had she only worn a frock. It was not just her saree but her talent in hosting that placed her on equal footing with them.Surinder was very fond of her and protective in some circumstances. Not to forget, Anita was one of the two girls introduced by Malini to them.

"Do you know out of two professors in History department one has been absenting himself for almost four months now for illness?" Surinder triggered the bomb on the table, expressing her concern for students.Shamim thought this was a question addressed to Ratnakar; he didn't seem perturbed over a professor's absence.

Ratnakar who was confused for a moment replied:"Yes. So?"

"The students in my class are restive about Principal's crass negligence. In other classes their anger has reached a boiling point." Surinder defined the situation.

"College unit of Students' Federation must sit today to discuss this problem. It's not that the students' union is not aware of it but it takes time for seriousness to sink in." Ratnakar argued.

"Wait. I haven't finished yet. The Chhatra Parishad which you consider as siding the administration usually had already stolen a march over you in that it had already placed a memorandum to the Principal with 100 signatures of concerned students demanding regular classes in history immediately." Surinder Kaur was a leader with her ears to the ground. Ratnakar was surprised at this bit of information.

"If what you say is true, and there's no doubt now it is, we've lost ground in organization to them. We should have been the first to raise this issue." Ratnakar gravely said.

"Ratnakar da, you don't seem to realize how tense the situation at this moment is."Anita who was more interested in the serious aspect of a thing than its lighter side said," I can tell you that there are four copies of two history books in the library whereas the number of students seeking them is over 150. Actually, from the students' point of view the college is doing nothing for them; and students' union less than nothing. This is the reality which you've ignored. Or else you'd have acted much earlier."

That these two girls were capable of feeling the students' pulse became evident and this impressed Ratnakar no end. They weren't just two among the crowd; but thinkers in their own right.

"What kind of action do you expect from us, the union?" Ratnakar asked Anita to elicit her views.

"Why, if you can't do anything, you can at least shout slogans. Write posters. Lead a deputation to Principal's chamber." She replied promptly, words flowing from her lips non-stop as if from a fall.

'It's easier pronounced than implemented." Shamim intervened to say:"It has been our experience that at the appointed time and place for deputation students shy away from joining it for fear or for just anything. But this won't stop us from doing precisely what you said. It's possible we may hold the meeting right today." Shamim, coming back to his laughing self, softly said,"And thank you for enlightening us."

Outside, after the relentless heat, it was the turn of rain to express its frenzy. The road was deserted except for a stray motor vehicle creeping cautiously in the thick rain with visibility almost nil. Ratnakar looked at his friends. They were busily enjoying their coffee oblivious of the rain outside. He extended his hand for his cup.

CHAPTER TWENTY FIVE

It would appear that Ratnakar enjoyed his life with abandon at college studying, chitchatting, immersing in students' union activities, keeping aloft Students' Federation's banner and generally frolicking with mixed groups in canteens. Yes, this was one side of his existence. And yet every moment that he spent in the college was not without the thought of the Party which was struggling against the exploiting classes, against the crippling impact of the food policy relentlessly pursued by the Congress Government. It was not a mere theoretical issue with him. He felt like others of the district the debilitating effect of scarcity of food commodities.

Ratnakar's father, who had a sweetmeat shop which was the only source of family's income, felt disturbed when suddenly sugar and maida (fine flour) began to disappear from the market throwing the business in turmoil. It could survive only if it paid more than double the normal price of these items in the black-market. Who said food articles were not available? They were, but at black-market price, at a premium.

By 1956 a hand-picked municipality Congress-style was in place at Kadampur and its vice-chairman was authorized to issue coupons of the quotas to licensed shop-owners. The wholesale dealers having agreed to give part of their commodities in controlled price used to distribute sugar or flour or both to those who produced the coupons issued by the authority. Ratnakar had to go to this vice-chairman to obtain his coupon who would try to lessen his quota from 40 seers (kg) to 35 or 30 seers. The next destination after this unnamed experience was the distributor's outlet where he could always tell him to come after some time or the next day. However humiliating, he had to do the job and he did it because it was an issue of survival.

The Gujarati distributor, Karamchand Dharamchand Modi commented as soon as he spotted Ratnakar walking towards him with a coupon: "God alone knows wherefrom these people appear." Even though he heard the contemptuous remark, he ignored it. Extending the coupon towards him Ratnakar said politely, "I came yesterday with this coupon. You told me to come today."

"So?"

"Please see it. In place of distributor your name is written. And the quantity stated is 35 seers. Please give me that."

"But I won't give you any maida (flour), quota or no quota." The Gujarati distributor suddenly announced. Perhaps the quantity on the coupon revealed his economic status prompting him to think Ratnakar could be dismissed this way.

"You refuse to give me my quota?" Ratnakar was also raising his voice. His servants and some outsiders collected there by that time.

"Yes I refuse to give maida on the basis of this coupon." The distributor, Karamchand Dharamchand Modi, with his tall personality could without any doubt overawe anybody, not to speak of a small denomination shopkeeper.

"Then write on it that you refuse to give the quota because the vice-chairman wouldn't believe my statement about your negating it." Ratnakar told him plainly.

Modi was in a rage and considered himself not less than an Alexander. He looked at him with venomous eyes and wrote on the coupon:" I refuse it.", and signed.

Ratnakar went straight to the Party office to report this incident which was an insult to all his being the like of which he never went through ever in his life. He was fuming with anger inside. What the vice-chairman would feel about the distributor's dishonoring his coupon was yet to be seen. Harinarayan Mishra heard the episode straight from him along with other comrades, and comprehending the seriousness of the issue, promptly telephoned the chairman of Kadampur Municipality who expressed surprise at the incident and promised to take action as soon as the refused coupon was returned to the vice-chairman.

When Ratnakar met the vice-chairman the same day after some hours to hand him over the coupon, his reaction was:"I'll take action against him for insulting me." He gave him a fresh coupon writing another distributor's designation—one Mr. Agarwal's—and the harrowing tale seemingly ended with the dealer complying with the order, but—and this is a significant but—not before Ratnakar was given the subtle impression that the rich and the poor do not compare. How did he convey this impression? That would make another story. Comrade Sengupta in a different context in the district committee office once told him:" You can't be a good communist without hating the class enemy, without self-cultivation and study."This ego-crushing event was sufficient to make him a communist even if he was not one before this happening.

Ratnakar had to skip college classes often to collect roti-packets from Party sympathizers and others for those sitting on dharna at Midnapore collectorate demanding food policy change, among other things. Since the Party at Kadampur was still too small and not in a position to send jathas (groups) it contributed its mite to this movement by sending food-packets for those engaged in sit-ins.

As Ratnakar's attention was divided between college and the Party, he had taken perhaps a little more time than others to understand the method adopted by food scarcity perpetrators. From 1956 onward food movement became an annual occurrence in the State and Ratnakar with other comrades collected food-packets from their specific areas and in the process learned how the exploiting classes' method worked and why the food scarcity or famine was called man-made by the Party. Once when they met at a place chosen by Nabeen Mitra during this movement he tried to explain this phenomenon: "Rice mill-owners, jotedars and hoarders combined together to play the game of exploiting the cultivators and the poor people who were propelled into the web produced by them. Despite some laws against hoarders no action is ever taken against them."

"But why?" someone asked.

"Because hoarders themselves are Congressmen. A minister of state of this Government was recently found to have bags of rice in his warehouses much in excess of the ceiling. Who could take action against him?"Nabeen Mitra continued:" They're the most exploited—the marginal peasants and the landless—but they vote the Congress as dictated by the trio. Such is their all-pervasive stranglehold over the rural poor. The victory of Congress is thus ensured from rural Bengal."

The extent of exploitation could be gauged from the steadily dawning fact of hunger taking the huge shape of famine in W.Bengal. As it grew grim and became an issue of sheer survival people organized themselves into a "Committee to Combat Famine "under CPI. Later it was okayed by some other parties. Ratnakar felt the intensification of class struggle though it was still a rural phenomenon from his point of view. But famine broke every barrier and Food Movement of 1959 proved a turning point in W. Bengal's history of class struggle, with urban areas coming in its sweep.

On 31 August a huge demonstration was organized in Calcutta by the Kisan Sabhas to draw the State Government's attention to famine conditions and for immediate arrangement of food for the hungry. Who were the demonstrators? Small peasants, village womenfolk with babies in arms, office workers, high school students and factory hands. An estimated 300,000 people marching in columns on the roads of the Capital demanded an end to destitution. But what did they get for all their labor in the evening's darkness? They were cordoned off in the first move of police plan. Calcutta was witness to how they resorted to violent action on the unarmed hapless hungry people without even so much as a warning.

80 starving people were killed with sheer sticks by police, with no bullets fired. Nothing could beat this carnage, this dehumanized frenzy of the Government. In the confusion that followed in the darkness 3000 were injured, while 1000 were found missing. There was more to it than these gory, chilling truths.

Even the next day, September 1, when the students came out in strength to protest this genocide, they were fired. The ruling class was determined to let loose a reign of terror and repression with troops called out even in districts of Bengal.

If Kadampur Party office looked deserted, the reason was police hunt for senior leaders or anyone who they thought was proactive. Every comrade was given instruction to avoid arrest as far as possible but continue to meet at designated places, write and paste posters, and distribute handbills from underground.

Ratnakar was this time up against a problem he couldn't tackle all alone. Jayanta Naha helped him in difficult situations by giving him fail-proof advice but going to his house in the prevailing context whether during day or night would amount to risking his arrest,supposing he were at home, because his house must be under vigilance of intelligence branch. His parents told him to stay at home and remain confined and nothing would happen to him. They'd say to the police even if they came there their son did nothing. What innocence! The police would throw a dossier at them telling them their son at this time and date was present when workers of a factory got violent in the manager's office, was inciting workers against police or collecting subscription for CPI at workshop gate or attending a secret meeting to help peasants struggling against a jotedar (lord of big farming lands). Ratnakar thought that it would be a downright idiocy to remain at home and embroil his family in it. It wasn't that they were not afraid of police. And yet they did not want him to leave home. Suddenly it struck one of his parents that there was a family up at a place called Traffic in the railway area who could provide him shelter for some days. This family was interested in marrying into Ratnakar's family—they had a son and a daughter.

Marry anyone was their proposal, and the negotiation was going on precisely at that time. Ratnakar agreed to this suggestion but disappeared from his house from that night on without leaving his next address.

CHAPTER TWENTY SIX

Since the time Ratnakar joined 3rd year (1st year BA) he had begun to detect a tendency on the part of the Principal to be partial to Chhatra Parishad leaders which became evident in his going out of the way to meet some of their demands, significant or otherwise, promptly ; in his giving a patient hearing to the narration of their problems ; in his departing from the standard practice of admitting students on accepted criteria to permitting admission of ineligible students on their recommendations. It wasn't his imagination: he could lengthen the list. Not all of these meets or confabulations between CP and the Principal, it was understood, were open. Clearly there was some unseen force which was making him act the way he did. Though these acts did not fit in with his reputation as a scholar and administrator, the reality could not be ignored. And that was the rub.

It so happened that All-India Students' Federation gave a strike call next week in support of their charter of demands based on reports from different State organizations. Shreya, Malini and some others were enthusiastic about making the strike a success. They had called students under their influence to the swimming pool side to hold the meeting to discuss the strategy for strike. It was supposed to be a small group meeting but the gathering became unexpectedly bigger. When

Ratnakar was speaking to his audience taking one by one demand from the charter, some messenger came from the Principal's office and said to Ratnakar :"Sir is calling you. You can't hold this meeting here."

"But this isn't a meeting. We're merely discussing our problems. This does not disturb any class." Someone among the students argued.

"I can only say Principal is very angry. Ratnakar must see him immediately." The messenger affirmed.

"You've conveyed Principal's message. Now you can go." Ratnakar said politely but firmly."Please don't mind. I've no quarrel with you."

Ratnakar did not meet the Principal. He continued explaining the demands but shortened the matter. The attitude, however, hardened on both sides.

Malini remarked in Pulin da's cabin:"Principal's cleverness is nowhere as evident as in the making of students' union constitution which could be manipulated and interpreted to bail him out of any embarrassment. It's a pity you couldn't bring any change after last year's election." It was a fact no time or thought was given to amending the constitution to meet present requirements during the last year. The election of the vice-president from students for which only senior students were eligible to be candidates drew political attention much beyond the boundary of the college. Considering the smallness of the town which depended entirely on the railway for its sustenance,it was not surprising, particularly after the emergence of the CPI as a political force in the non-railway part of the town, people attached considerable importance to this event for which the whole student community constituted one big electoral college. During this period the college went in an intellectual ferment and the people were eager to know what the reading generation thought about the current affairs. They watched which way the wind swayed—left or right.

Shreya added to Malini's remark:" The constitution is delightfully vague about the mode of this election and its timing. Isn't it?"

"If girl students continue to be deprived of their voting rights in this manner what'll happen to Ratnakar da who is going to be our vice-presidential candidate. We must do something to change 3pm-8pm to 10am-8pm time to facilitate girl students to use their voting rights." Surinder made this strong plea.

Malini said,"But first things first. The question of his election would come after the withdrawal of Principal's notice of suspension. Talk of the next day."

The next day it was arranged, to begin with, that Ratnakar would move from room to room and make use of the time between the end of a class and the beginning of the next to appeal to students to help make the all-India strike of Students' Federation a grand success specifically pointing out that the realization of the demands would benefit them immensely. When he entered a class-room as soon as the prof's lecture was over, he requested the students to allow him to speak a few words to them; most of the students remained stuck to their benches which implied the groundwork was already laid by SF supporters. But he had only 10 minutes to convincingly explain demands to them. Ratnakar was precisely doing this with utmost concentration when the Principal stormed into the class.

"Ratnakar, you cannot address the students in this manner in the class-room. This is breaking discipline. I ask you to immediately leave the class."Principal shouted at him.

"But I've not broken any discipline. As soon as I see a professor coming I'll leave the room. I've no intention of disturbing the class in any manner." Ratnakar was justifying his act, standing his ground.

"I won't allow you to propagate your ideology in the class-room. You've already broken discipline by not complying with my order. Am I the Principal or you? What should be done in the class-room is my province." Principal was shuddering with rage as he was not accustomed to having a counter argument ever.

"But Sir, I'm requesting you for a little democracy in the democratic country." Ratnakar thought this a strong point in his favour."And so long as I don't disturb any class, I don't break any discipline."

"You've challenged the Principal and breached college discipline. Action will be taken against you." He left the room in a huff.

The stunned class recovered from the shock a moment or two after Principal's departure. The situation for Ratnakar completely altered and the students dispersed in silence.

True to his words the Principal did not delay in taking action: he issued a notification to the effect that Ratnakar was suspended from the college for a period of 20 days with immediate effect. No sooner was it put on the notice-board than the commotion started. To say that students were not terrified by this bombshell of an announcement would be an error of judgment but it was equally true the fear was short-lived. It was replaced by a sober determination to fight. The rival Congress—affiliated Chhatra Parishad was watching students' reaction with keen interest, concealing their glee at Ratnakar's discomfiture. But the arbitrariness in the Principal's measure against Ratnakar was too glaring to be missed by the dullest intellect. In some students' view nothing could be more autocratic, authoritarian and undemocratic than the punishment handed over by the Principal to him.

It was Jayanta Naha who first broke the fear line by organizing a procession in the college premises and its corridors shouting slogans against the Principal's unjust action. "Withdraw notice against Ratnakar ", "Hands off democratic rights of students "were the slogans along with "Students' Federation Zindabad "that were raised in the procession.

Malini,Shreya,Sujata,Surinder were not far behind in organizing a second procession predominated by girls shouting similar slogans. Before they organized the procession some of them came to him in a gesture of building his confidence and telling him that they would be with him till the last, come what might. All this generated a strange feeling in Ratnakar. This was a movement which was led entirely by others up to this moment.

As a leader of certain experience Ratnakar felt Principal would not have acted solely on the basis of immediate surcharged emotion in this manner without some calculation. Jayanta Naha and girl comrades' response to Principal's patently unjust move was in the right direction but he feared this might still fall short of persuading,forcing the Principal to retrace his obnoxious step. He decided to apprise senior leaders of the Party of the grave issue of their direct confrontation on a political plane with the highest authority of the college immediately. He left for the Party office after telling Naha that he was going to meet Com Harinarayan Mishra and others for their advice. They could hold the fort without him.

He found Harinarayan Mishra busy as expected with schedule of programmes lined up for him as MLA but when he heard of his suspension he stopped in the middle of his work and looked at him strangely. What he said was stranger still: So you've done this time around something which attracted Principal's action. Well done, brave heart. The Party is with you and since Principal has chosen this confrontation with us directly, we shall fight."

"We're fighting with him at college level. Com Naha and Malini are at the moment leading processions right inside the college campus." Ratnakar informed Mishra da. "But it appears unless there's some powerful intervention from outside Principal might not withdraw the notice."

"I'm going out right now." Mishra da said. "But you call all those students who can come here in the meeting. The Party will take a decision as nothing is more important at this moment as your suspension."

"To complicate matters students' union election falls within the period of my suspension." The last sentence from Ratnakar will make Mishra da think of the grave implications of the present issue.

"We shall discuss this also in the meeting in the evening." Mishra da said before departing.

CHAPTER TWENTY SEVEN

Ratnakar was under the impression that his mission of informing the senior Party comrades would take a chunk of substantial time because for all he knew they might not be available in the office when he reached there. In which case he had to wait for them and the wait, who could tell, might be prolonged. It therefore gave him a measure of satisfaction that he had been able to accomplish the job within half an hour of reaching the office and was free now to go back to the college where the battle was.

He felt hungry but frankly he didn't have the stomach for it since the process of eating, particularly at home, was time-consuming and time was precisely the commodity he didn't have at that moment. He must return to the college immediately and join his friends and let the thought of food go to hell for once. He ran the cycle furiously and covered the 2-mile + stretch to college within 15 minutes.

Naha was surprised to see him back so soon."Did you inform Mishra da about the happening? Wasn't there any other senior comrade there?"He sounded alarmed.

"I talked to Mishra da and others too."He dispelled Naha's concerns and anxieties and then narrated what passed between him and the other comrades.

Updated, Naha said,"Some protesters must go to the Party office, particularly those from Netajipally area; to put their views in the meeting. But a few must remain here to continue the movement in the night section."

While they talked about not letting the thread of the agitation break till the night students came the scene of the day college presented a satisfactory aspect of the story in that all classes looked deserted. Processionists continued to shout slogans without showing any sign of fatigue. Those who didn't join them strolled in groups of threes and fours.

It was a measure of enthusiasm and a commitment to ideology that Malini,Shreya,and Surinder Kaur and the recent find Swapna Jana,who were not expected to face commerce students,also sat in the meeting to chalk out a strategy to persuade them to help their cause of protesting the undemocratic and authoritian suspension of Ratnakar. There was good reason to believe that night students would be discerning enough to find fault with the Principal's unwarranted action. But political matters are not judged on the basis of their merit, truth or righteousness and Ratnakar's suspension could be politicized the moment Chhatra Parishad came out in support of the Principal. Which would mean divided opinion in terms of majority-minority. Ratnakar and his friends could not avoid this prospect.

The next day,it was decided by the college SF unit, there would be a dharna in front of the Principal's office which was expected to be joined by about 100 students and,on day three, a strike call, in case the authority did not countermand the questionable notice even after the dharna, was given. A leaflet was accordingly prepared questioning the rationale of Principal's action and much more to be distributed among students before evening.

The sit-in drew a large number of girl students which indicated their growing consciousness about politics. This also symbolized at a different level their new-found language of protest against injustice. By noon the number of the participants increased and so the decibels. The sit-in looked more like a gherao than anything else.

The spontaneous support for Ratnakar put the injustice to him in so glaring a light that perhaps none could remain unaffected except the diehard sympathizers of Chhatra Parishad. There were others too of a different kind who despite detecting fault in the Principal confessed to their helplessness before him. Clearly, the whole of the college—ranging from the staff to administration to Chhatra Parishad—were aligned against him.

In a situation like this there was no way left but to fight hard to remain afloat. If there was any doubt lurking about polarization on political lines SF's leaflet, in Bengali and English, detailing Principal's arbitrary and high-handed acts including the latest firing shot, dispelled it. That he had been sitting over the just demands of students for about a year now stemmed from his ever-present hostile attitude. There was nothing in the printed leaflet that could cheer the head of the college.

Highly disturbed at the Principal's unsympathetic silence, a section of students decided to go at it hammer and tongs to make next day's strike a grand success. The sit-in was at once stopped to make necessary spadework for the real object. Only a few students were asked to come to the Party office.

Jayanta was too tired to go to the office straight from the college and wanted leave to be refreshed with a bath at home to feel fit for the meeting. Everybody agreed with him looking at his crumpled dress and perspiring face though their state was no different.

When Ratnakar found Jayanta waiting for him on the day of the strike, he was agreeably surprised as it was the first time he didn't have to wait for him to get into the dress for the occasion. Ratnakar would have opportunity to remember him not only as a helpful friend but also as a responsible leader. There was a freshness oozing out of him, and he looked a mass of bubbling energy, right then. They sped towards the waiting rickshaw.

Their antennae were up when they spotted Mustafa, the Chhatra Parishad leader, near the gate of the college which appeared closed. A dhoti-clad man was standing on the other side of the gate with the key along with a dozen others who resembled neither employees nor students guarding it. They got off the rickshaw and were moving towards the gate when some students came running towards them from nearby tea-stalls. Dulal was the first to speak to them:"Some strike-breakers had already entered into the college when the gate was open. I saw some staff members also getting inside it much before the college hours. The inside information is that Principal asked them to take the classes whatever be the number of students present. Just to break the strike."

"This is not a strike for the staff. Their attendance does not matter, but students' entry does. We must request them to come out of the classes." Jayanta said calmly, pondering the situation.

"Open the gate."Ratnakar shouted at the man who had the key of the lock.

"We shall not open the gate. Principal had ordered us not to allow you to enter the college as you are suspended from it." The reply was given by his companion who seemed to be the leader of the group manning it.

It was clear as day that the Principal in league with Chhatra Parishad had taken up position of confrontation much earlier than their arrival. Jayanta got furious at Principal's coming down to this level in which he didn't mind using outsiders to put obstruction in their way of entry in the college just to break the strike. The effect of all this was that the news of forcible stopping of Ratnakar and Jayanta and other strikers spread fast and in half an hour's time some 50 SF supporters rushed to the spot to strengthen the agitation.

"Open the gate." Jayanta commanded those standing on the other side of the strongly-built wooden gate with rods jutting skyward."This is a democratic movement; Principal cannot get the gate locked and bar Ratnakar or any other student in this manner."

"But we've orders not to allow Ratnakar inside the college. You can go back or continue your slogans. We're here to execute Principal's order. "The same man made this acid reply.

The other students continued the slogans in a rhythmic manner. Naha in the midst of the noise said to Ratnakar," We've to use force There's no way we can get in without doing something of this sort. "

"Agreed. Let's push it and break it." Ratnakar replied clearly.

Naha rushed back to the gate and started using force against it. The other students got the cue and the strength of students which doubled in the meantime clashed with that of a dozen or so mercenaries who tried to stop the wave of the ocean. It was a matter of minutes before the gate fell in two parts. Ratnakar's hands were on the gate just as Naha's but they somehow escaped falling along with the gate. There were minor injuries on both sides but the strikers didn't care. They were jubilant at the fall of the symbol of resistance and resumed their slogans and marched forward.

There were certainly some students in a couple of classes and the teachers were taking lessons. But as soon as they got wind of the breaking of the gate the students came out of the rooms, maybe, because of curiosity or fear or sheer shame. They might be Chhatra Parishad supporters for all one knew. But SF members were glad they didn't have to use persuasion or force to get them out of the classes. Considering mighty factors arrayed against them, the strike might be called a mild success so far as the day college was concerned.

The night section students were still quite a way off and might pose a problem as they always did in the past. But the breaking of the gate was a big story and it had its own message, even for commerce section. They decided to take rest before the Principal's office. The Principal this time did not come out to threaten them with disciplinary action. Those who were guarding the gate also couldn't be seen anywhere in the college. A strange silence seemed to grip the college.

But CP leaders were not exactly sitting idle, having failed during day to stop the strike from being a success it was. Sitting in the Congress office with senior leaders, they devised a strategy, as it transpired later, of sending their local leaders to homes of commerce students with the message to stay away from the strike in their future interest. They put pressure on them pointing out the fact the IB report might go against them or their parents.

As a result of their day-long labor many night students came to the college but when they saw the state of the college—broken gate lying along the sides, slogan-shouting students distributing leaflets to them— some of them preferred return to arguing with them. Those who stayed did go to the class-rooms only to find, instead of the lecturers, goats fastened to the teacher's tables.

CHAPTER TWENTY EIGHT

The period 1957-58 for Ratnakar as well as Kadampur College unit of AISF was an epoch of intense activities for building the organization to keep it in step with other mass organizations of the Party which were working tirelessly to increase their membership at the ground level. Naha and he were caught in the whirlwind of 1957-58 and had literally no time for their own studies. They had to meet students individually to motivate them to be members of SF. Not surprisingly not many were convinced of their arguments at the first encounter. Sometimes it took three or four sessions to bring them anywhere near a positive frame of mind.

Ratnakar was unlikely to forget an experience which shed an interesting light on the mental make—up of a special section of girls who considered themselves different from the common run of girls for no reason other than that they happened to have English medium high school background. Champa Kumari Singh, residing in south-side locality of this railway town, couldn't resist showing this vanity and made the other girls feel that she didn't belong to their set. "But she had other vivacious qualities," Bandana, her friend, defended her.

During his move to make as many SF members as possible before the district conference Ratnakar met Miss Singh along with her other friends and had the opportunity of requesting and persuading her to be a member of their organization. The talk with her was held in English. She evinced a keen interest in the organization's work and asked some questions unlike others, and when he turned his attention to another group in a move to leave her, she suddenly said distinctly,"I want to be a member of your organization. Tell me what I should do about it."

"Nothing much. You should fill this form up and sign it which will take four to 5 minutes and pay Re one only as membership fee for this year."Ratnakar, duly surprised, put the form printed both in English and Bengali in her hand.

He helped her complete the form, and when she took Re one from her little stylish purse and gave it to him, the words that involuntarily came to his lips were," Thank you." He proceeded to another group of first year students.

It was perhaps the next day that the unexpected happened. No sooner did he enter the college gate than came Miss Singh rushing to him as if from nowhere and confronted him with a piece of paper. She pushed it in his hand. She was standing, waiting there to precisely do this."I want to resign from your organization with immediate effect. My parents don't want me to associate with it." And she disappeared leaving him stunned and thinking. Was it the impulse in the first place that made her join the SF? But her resignation from it in this manner indicated the fear that was writ large in her eyes. She had the look of a terrorized soul.

There was a hilarious episode too in this drive concerning Dahareswar Basu who surprised Ratnakar and Durgapada Ghosh twice by slipping from their organization and making himself scarce forcing them to search him from place to place. His importance lay in the fact that he belonged to a jotedar (big land-owner) family but with progressive ideas of his own. He was acutely conscious of the wrongs done by his class to the poor and landless peasants. Consequently he was capable of influencing students, especially from rural background, as no one else among them could.

There was one more reason which enhanced his significance in the SF organization. He alone had the specific mechanism in his mind tucked away to devise strategies to take on the mighty forces represented by Barun Pahari and Anand Patra who belonged to well-known rich Congress families of Keshiary and wielded tremendous influence on rural students. Chhatra Parishad leaders did not have to approach them; the duo sought the town Congress office out and introduced themselves. One could guess from this the kind of loyalty they had for the Congress. There was nothing that could be said against their personalities because they were not fractious, never seen shouting at anyone. If anything they were sober, controlled, with their white dhoti and shirt emphasizing decency unlike their counterparts of the town.

But fight the SF must the CP. Only an ideological battle will help them penetrate this wall between them and rural students. Ratnakar and Durgapada Ghosh had to sit with Dahareswar Basu at many eating stalls including Kamala Cabin to remove his doubts about ideological stand of SF and CPI. All this might sound bizarre but wasn't this place full of wonders?

The membership drive aimed at electing and sending delegates from local units to district conference which in turn would send delegates to higher bodies. It was an opportunity for the newcomers to witness and participate in the democracy that prevailed in AISF.When the

Midnapur district conference was held at Kanthi, a Kanthi-based student, Purnendu Dasgupta was elected secretary, and Ratnakar assistant secretary.

This gave him a wider opportunity to interact with district leadership of the Party where he took issues of other college units apart from his own's.

When he was going through this stressful situation it was a relief to him to learn the day following the strike that the Principal had withdrawn by notification his order of suspension on him with immediate effect in the best interest of the college.

The news spread among students within minutes who heaved a victorious sigh of relief. The occasion was celebratory but Ratnakar put his feet down here. It was therefore peace, a jubilant peace that prevailed in the college.

He was sitting on the steps of a building which for some reason was not used for some days with his friends, some standing around him. He said, "I'd a plan."

"What?" asked Panchu? "Let me describe it in my own way. And don't butt in in the middle.

'Ratnakar went to the principal's office, stood at the door, said "May I come in, Sir.'

'Come in. Now what?

'I've come here to say I didn't mean to hurt you in any manner. And thank you for your kindness.' He left his office."

Surinder Kaur immediately reacted to it:" Forget this plan."

Miss Bhowmick said,"This isn't the time to be generous or modest.'

"What makes you think the fire we fought till yesterday has extinguished today with the withdrawal of suspension on you?"

Chanchal, the knight of the night brigade of commerce classes, said,"I agree with my friends' reactions. In view of the continuing undercurrent of hostility your view sounds enormously stupid."

So, there he was.

Clearly the SF was prepared to fight the battle to a conclusion even if the authorities persisted in their obstinacy till the election. His form for candidacy for vice-president could be rejected on the ground of being a defaulter! Such things were not unknown in the games politicians played. It was in this sense the withdrawal of suspension order on him was a relief.

Since the filing of nomination form was looked into by Naha, Chanchal and others he was assured of a safe passage.

But who was the Chhatra Parishad candidate for V-P? When his name was announced many were surprised. He was Sudhansu Sur, ten to 15 years senior to him, railway employee, only a step away from being promoted to coveted foreman's post in the workshop. With the principal being president as per the union constitution, Sur with his tall stature would make a nice impressive V-P if elected. How formidable was he as a candidate?

This was the area that touched Ratnakar and his followers. Once Chhatra Parishad labeled him Sudhansu Sur would lose all identities except the one given by it. In the ultimate analysis, the battle would be fought along political lines.

It was decided in one of the meetings that Ratnakar should be more visible in night section than he was so far without being provocative and keeping right to the right side of discipline.

There was no doubt about this election being one hell of an event that would be remembered for some time to come. Posters, banners, leaflets—the SF could match them. But when Mustafa joined the fray with wads of notes backing him, the picture for Sur drastically changed. Money had its own logic, attraction and force for night section students.

The election was held under the dated practice of 3 to 8 pm, unfavorable to girls. Two marked boxes were kept in a room, one for each candidate. The only thing that the CP and administration did not reckon was the girls' determination to vote. They succeeded in their objective.

At the last count of votes, when the excitement was at its peak, Ratnakar was leading by 24 votes. Chhatra Parishad demanded recounting of votes.

When the recounting was in progress, Ratnakar detected an anomaly in the official paper showing total number of valid voters. But the ballot papers from the two boxes just counted far exceeded that number. Naha also got smell of a foul play. He allowed the second counting to pass as he wanted to be certain if all the papers had the Principal's signature. They had.

Ratnakar was the first to say to authorized election officials:" There were more ballot papers in two boxes than total valid voters in college. There is foul play in it. All contained Principal's signature according to you. I demand repoll. Seal the boxes when we are here."

CP tried to blame SF. The commotion began. Slogans against principal's conspiracy had begun to dagger into midnight's air.

CHAPTER TWENTY NINE

The election for vice-president was held on 5th of this month with the process continuing up to 8 pm after which the boxes were sealed in the manner election officials deemed fit. The tired officials had nothing to do after this except to deposit the boxes in the Principal's office at a designated spot under lock and key. The key had to be handed over to the Principal. The counting of votes started on 6th towards evening.

Finding of more ballot papers, all valid, than total voters of the college was an unprecedented event by any reckoning. The act was outright condemnable, indefensible and when all indications pointed to the Principal's complicity in it the blame was laid at the SF's door as if the office was run by it and not by the Principal. But this was what politics was all about.

The incident bamboozled, outraged, disappointed SF supporters in no small measure. They felt frustrated because whatever they did could be undone by the authorities in this manner. Out of this frustration was brewing a sense of fight with them to a finish.

The CPI took it in the spirit of a Congress challenge in the form of Principal and Com Harinarayan Mishra and others agreed to take the issue outside the college. A program was taken to hold a convention of prominent citizens, academicians and students immediately to

RAJ JAIN

focus the scandal which had shaken faith in the highest authority of the college. Com Mishra, after several attempts, had been able to snatch an interview with the District Magistrate who did not believe his version. Not that Mishra da bothered about him. The law and order situation would make him change his view.

The other scene was a slowly gathering cloud of thunder. If not all, some super rich men—in local parlance,capitalists—united behind the Principal and the Congress. With so much in the fire of night commerce students the bulk of whom came from the railway workshop, the scandal reached its shores also.

Never before in the history of the college was witnessed a war of leaflets, posters on a scale as stupendous as this. But in 48 hours' time CP seemed to be losing this battle of nerves as their number visibly dwindled while the SF' increased if the size of Principal's *gherao was taken into consideration. No classes were held during this period.

And what was the list of demands this time?

1) An enquiry committee to probe how ballot papers came out of Principal's custody. Guilty to be punished.
2) Re-election of V-P
3) Counting of votes immediately after election
4) No victimization of anybody on any ground
5) Democratization of students' union constitution

The Principal called Ratnakar and others spearheading the students' agitation for a meeting on the third day after the botched counting of votes to find a solution to the continuing problem. Obviously some behind-the-scene work was done which resulted in his come-down. Though the meeting was held in the first hours of the college, his *gherao was not weakened.

Except for who would constitute members of the enquiry committee, Principal agreed to all the demands. V-P election would be held like class representative election. The girl students would be able to enjoy their franchise in their own classes, a right largely denied in 3pm-8pm system. Ratnakar said at the end of the meeting," So, do we understand, Sir, that you have accepted all our demands?"

"Yes, I've accepted all the demands. In fact, I'm soon going to issue a notification for fresh election of vice-president under changed rules which would be incorporated in the S.U. constitution later." Principal replied, his voice reflecting a change in his attitude.

"As soon as we get a signed copy of your acceptance, we shall sit to call off the movement." Naha stood up in a gesture to finish the meeting. Arun Chatterjee perhaps wanted to say something but he thought the better of it for now.

As soon as the notification was glued on the notice board, Ratnakar busied himself putting election machinery in place. It was one thing to agitate for demands or even collect students on a wave of sentiment; it was another to ensure their attendance on the day of election. Their complacency might prove hazardous.

With the college returning to normal, the picture of students' was becoming clearer. Naha said to Ratnakar:"Though we apparently won the ruined election, CP was not defeated."

"If we don't work harder things may not fall our way in this prestige fight."Ratnakar was speaking thoughtfully.

"The Party must use all its resources. It must tap its workshop influence, however little it might have."

"That they will. But will it be sufficient to make us the winner is the question." Naha expressed his doubt.

The re-election for V-P was held class-wise for the first time reminding everybody that this was the occasion for the girls to smile. It was peaceful, orderly and swift setting a trend. There was no surprise when Ratnakar was elected V-P at the end of the second counting which was demanded by CP but the margin of 27 only rankled many SF supporters. Ratnakar was the only person to have won the same election twice. The significance of this victory could not be dismissed just as the real strength of C P now could not be ignored.

Sulekha Pandit,the tall thin second year girl,with a tooth jutting out adding a beauty ti her smile,said :"But I'm not pleased with victory merely by 27 votes."

"Who is?" Malini was quick on the take. "We expected better after facts established the immorality of theft of ballot papers against Principal and CP."

"The myth of morality stands exposed. There's nothing like this in election."Sulekha said ruefully.

For Ratnakar it was a lesson. But by the time the next V-P election came he wouldn't be around here as he'd be appearing then at the final BA Exam, with his date with the college over forever.

While they sat near the pool analyzing the election in a relaxed manner, groups of tittering girls passed by them making a little more noise than usual. What was remarkable was the addition of soft laughter, a release of a pent-up feeling, to their movement.

"Well, Malini, now tell me. Are these girls joyous about the SF's V-P victory by 27 votes?" Ratnakar asked. She started thinking about the reply.

Ratnakar said further:"If all of them voted the SF, the margin should have exceeded 27. The hilarity in them is all-pervasive. How do you explain this jocundity?"

"All of them might not have voted SF. But rest assured, they're damned well pleased to get the opportunity to vote in comfort this time in their own classes with all the assurance." Malini replied."But wait,Swapna is coming in that group. We shall stop her and find out what she has to say about it."

Even before Swapna got the signal to stop she shouted as soon as she came within hearing distance:" We're going to celebrate our victory."

"But . . ." Malini intercepted her.

"Not Ratnakar da's victory, I said 'our victory'." Swapna clarified.

"Invite them to Kamala Cabin and they'll understand." One from her group who was jiggling all the while said.

"We're going to commemorate the newly won freedom to vote for V-P election. "said Swapna," This was a French Revolution for us. " The spirit was infectious. Ratnakar Malini,Pandit stood up because they couldn't resist the charm.

When an event of momentous significance was happening and history was being created in college what was Chameli Chatterjee doing ? Wasn't it a wonderful thought for him ? When he was suspended and the college was in the embrace of a movement she was not to be seen which was stranger still. Can indifference go to this level? One snatch of news though came his way, much later, that she did participate in a group led by Durgapada Ghosh collecting support for him. This did not make any sense then.

It gave some burn to his heart. But, frankly, what did he do himself to earn sympathy in adversity from her ? He was too busy, too absorbed in his work that he never found it convenient to attempt to follow, search or hunt her as others did. He must be in the hold of love before he could think of running after her. Though the idea of love was yet to form in his heart, his heart ached for her.

He felt he was sinking and darkness seemed to cover all his being.

"Ratnakar da, what'd you like to have ?" It was a blurred picture of Swapna Jana for a moment that came to his view.

"Hot*pakoda and coffee if you please." Though they came here 20 minutes ago, it seemed an eternity.

CHAPTER THIRTY

W hen there was nothing in the atmosphere of joy's spring to suggest a life beyond this life, he got an intimation from Pradip Santra, his classmate for a while, who died when they barely stepped into the second year. Santra, a budding poet, who snuffed his own life, was now a denizen of the other world. About him, he remembered, what his close friend Panchu Gopal Das once said to him:"He writes better poetry than I do. He has cultivated a maturity which I lack. But you won't understand it. It's Bengali." The last sentence was a dig at Ratnakar but was not meant to be harsh. and was far from being unfriendly. They had laughed it out together.

Santra used to recite or sing a line or two of his poems between the interregnum of two classes and was a non-interfering, introspective kind of chap with a body, quite strangely, as sturdy as a soldier's. And yet his fiancée, a belle of his neighboring village, reportedly, stopped him in the middle of his advances and rejected him. What actually happened between them was still shrouded in a thick smog of mystery but the fact, however, was his attractive talents went utterly in vain. Perhaps unable to bear the shock he committed suicide.

Death was an imposing reality, no doubt, but why should it interfere with his celebration of life? Is this thought a premonition of something dirty, or like so many stupid things of life,nothing ?He had to force the thought away from his mind to participate in the fun around him. Pradip Santra wasn't very close to Ratnakar and something of a recluse and yet his death even after a year came back to torment him. Often he would find him sitting all alone in an abandoned class-room staring blankly through the window. Obviously he valued his privacy more than his friendship. Boys with this kind of forbidding nature didn't make many friends. Not surprisingly he had only one friend, Panchu, who hovered around him most of the time he was at college.

Pradip wouldn't talk like his age but more like an aged or experienced person which would make his listeners uncomfortable. It was therefore not astonishing when he chose an unnatural death, not many were curious about him. On the contrary, they avoided talking about him.

But Ratnakar's curiosity was whetted, despite himself. Was the girl also in love with him as he was in love with her? It appeared the smog covered this area after the question was framed. His charitable guess was that Santra rushed to a conclusion when he should have waited for the girl to unfold her mind in a world that had many unexpected turns for her. He must have misinterpreted her signals. But, wait, why was he guessing about the cause of the girl's rejection when Santra alone had the exclusive privilege to judge the signals emanating from her.

Death, to poets, was not a horrible concept or fearful event, but something which they cherished to taste and therefore called it by soft names as the poet John Keats did, didn't he ? He should better stop thinking about Pradip Santra and his death the contemplation of which surely would lead him to astray. However much he tried to jettison this wheel of thought, it returned to him with a force.

What about Tina Bhattacherjee—the irrepressible, brilliant student, who should have been here celebrating SF victory but was now lost to the world. Ratnakar had yet to meet an emotional creature like Tina. Perhaps it was written somewhere in her genetic code to embrace a violent death. When, after a prolonged courtship, she was informed by her boyfriend, Sukhendu, that he was getting off to US and that it was unlikely he would ever return to India, she got confused, then mad at him and then at everything. She committed suicide the third day after the shock. It was understood she lost all her senses before her death. When she was hanging herself from the ceiling fan of her parent's railway quarter, it was doubtful whether she was aware of what she was doing. Sukhendu was not really in love with Tina as later revelations suggested. Perhaps he could have avoided being an agent of her death. He went to US to learn commerce.

Ratnakar was dimly aware that he was sitting in Kamala Cabin with Swapna Jana beside him, with his eyes open and ears shut to the noise around him. He was slowly coming back to himself from the reverie.

"Your coffee and pakoda have been appropriated. Let me order one more for you."Swapna said to him.

"Let him have them. I can wait."

"Not 'Let him'. Make it 'Let her have them' if it's English." Swapna corrected him with a sense of pride and got up to give a fresh order for Ratnakar.

He decided he wouldn't fall in any amorous relation with any girl if it ended up in tragedy like the ones that struck his mind a few moments ago. Love was a bundle of inscrutable emotions and one just didn't know where it would end,if it ever ended, in the dark pit. He imagined a perpetual novice swimming love's pond the water of which was changing its depth. No, he wouldn't fall in love with any girl. Did he have Chameli in mind when he argued against getting into any emotional entanglement with any girl? He concluded he didn't want more from life on this score than what he was getting then.

After the boy set his coffee and plateful of pakoda on the table, she sat at her place.

"What are you waiting for now?" She asked him curiously.

"And what about you?" Ratnakar asked her politely

"Oh." She extended her hand to take a big globe of pakoda from his plate and said,"The same items are coming for me too." She started laughing. Was anything comparable to this genuine laughter ? He ruminated about it taking a solid pakoda. The hot coffee,he hoped, wouldn't allow him relapse into the mood of reflection on suicide.

It was bad enough to get into the morbid state of mind : it would be worse being the cause of disturbance to others who were enjoying life with abandon. He looked at Swapna who was making some knowing gesture to one of her friends, then peered at some other girls and boys who were busily eating or talking. Indeed they were sharing their ecstasy at the election victory.

He couldn't resist the thought that perhaps he wouldn't be here in any future celebration of any kind sharing the rapture with friends as this was the last before his final examination, which was only three months hence.

A coffee later Ratnakar felt like throwing away Albert Camus' thought (An Absurd Reasoning) :"There's but one truly serious philosophical problem, and that is suicide. Judging whether life is worth living amounts to answering the fundamental question of philosophy. " in the nearest dustbin.

Vainly did his eyes search for Chameli in this little crowd of revelers. Though he wasn't really imagining her participating in there, it pained him nevertheless to acknowledge that she was absent. If it was some kind of revelation of his infatuation for her, so be it. And involuntarily the word "Dream" escaped his lips.

"Did you call me?" Swapna turned her head towards him promptly.

Well . . . ." Ratnakar just glided.

"It was English translation. But it was still me." Swapna was curious why he called her, if he really did.

"Well . . . if involuntarily the word 'rose' had slipped from me would you still feel that concerned?" He suddenly stopped.

"Now what's this? From "dream' to 'rose', Ratnakar da, you are getting stranger." She continued,"So when you uttered "dream" it was not meant for me?"She was surprised. He did not answer this question. Everything was so obvious. Ratnakar was wondering whether she hadn't already made some advance in her relationship with him being the initiator of small things here and there.

Could she ever replace Chameli? He immediately dispelled this thought because the reality was he wouldn't be here just after three months. Secondly, he didn't visualize her in the frame of Chameli who had many admirers even among the staff and Swapna was just a tyro in the First year class with innocence as her only property

Suddenly they heard the sound of the breaking of glass dishes somewhere.

"Let me find out what happened?"Swapna jumped to her feet. Was it necessary for her to discover the reason for the sound, but she rushed to the scene. This was Swapna. This was also time for the breakup of the party.

CHAPTER THIRTY ONE

As vice-president of students' union Ratnakar hadn't much of a role to play as it was general secretary-centred but a greater role was cut for him in the organization with accretion of new strength and prestige which the post brought him. Class-representative election that followed the v-p's election saw a crest-fallen, wounded and yet-to-recover CP which proved no match to an active, enthusiastic, confident SF. Naha was chosen general-secretary of the Union which signaled a point of departure for Ratnakar in one sense. He was now left free to study, prepare for coming BA examination. Naha was a boy of proven caliber in matters of organization and could run all affairs without Ratnakar, at college level, that is. Except that he needed goading and imploration now and then at party level.

Ratnakar went to the library to borrow books, especially on economics, as he needed to understand some basic points to be able to answer questions on this subject. Without the text-books he felt he was at sea in front of some questions as he missed some important classes. In the library he could get only one book meeting his requirement though he was eligible for two according to rules. This was not something new for Ratnakar. Most students had similar experience of disappointment in the library. In fact he was lucky to get one book which could give just what he wanted.

Ratnakar cycled his way back to his tin-roofed small room, called study, attached to his house to find out whether he was fit to sit in the examination or not. He had the option to drop this year just as Jayanta did last year only to seek admission afresh in Honors in Economics as a first year student. The fact of the matter was that Kadampur College got affiliation in Economics Honors' teaching from Calcutta University that year and was in need of a respectable number of students to prove its viability.Jayanta glided in with no questions asked. But Ratnakar couldn't do what he did for the simple reason that he knew next to nothing about the *Dismal Science*. There was,however, one more reason why he couldn't drop the exam this year. It was that the act would send a wrong message to students. Engaging in union or Students Federation activities and studies do not go together. It would establish they were contradictory to each other.

To say there were no instances of it, assuming Jayanta Naha's case as exception because Honors subject would be an elevating and alluring proposition for anybody in any case, would be wrong. To make a long story short Ratnakar himself abhorred the idea of dropping. In the back of his mind, it was possible to conjecture, were the conditions of his family which were not what they should be at that time.

Ratnakar was very close to two of his friends in matters of study—Ramji Dubey and Bhaskar Rao. Though they were quite friendly to him and sympathetic to his cause for his sake, they preferred studies to any other act that distinguished them from him sharply. One day when the weather was nice and cycling could be comfortable he went to Dubey's place which was some kind of a Government quarter where he lived with his elder brother who worked in Post & Telegraph department. They cooked their own food and lived a Spartan life which was obvious from the room's look which had nothing in furniture's name except two cots. He spent one hour with Dubey discussing topics, exchanging notes. At the end of the session Dubey declared that he was not only fit to appear at the exam but was likely to get more marks than many. That was what he needed—encouragement.

He came back from him with determination to immerse himself in studies as he realized nothing could be achieved in this field without a passion for it. But all this evaporated the moment he faced an unnerving reality at home. When he entered a silence greeted him and he found his father lying on bed with his mother and sister fanning him with hand-fans and two younger brothers washing his head with wet towels. He was coming home after closing the shop for afternoon rest and lunch as usual but sunrays proved too much for his blood pressure and he was on the point of falling in the midway when a known person noticed him and helped him come here. Ratnakar retreated on his cycle without any further delay to a dispensary near their shop which was fortunately open but the doctor's chair was empty. He couldn't wait to be more civil and started shouting:" Doctor Babu, doctor babu. "

"What's this? Don't you know the dispensary is closed at this hour?"The doctor who could not ignore the shrill call shouted back from inside the house at the back of the dispensary."Come at 6 pm."He added with a tone of finality.

"But this is an emergency, Dr Babu. Please come for some minutes." Ratnakar persisted making his tone pitiable.

"But I was undressing for bath." he said with disgust.

"Please doctor. I wouldn't have disturbed you hadn't it been an emergency."

"Who are you? Are you Ratnakar ?"

"Yes, doctor. I'm Ratnakar."

"Wait. I'm coming."

He could recognize him from his voice. He knew Ratnakar was studying in college and was glad about it as he respected education a lot. Since the doctor examined his father on many other occasions in the past he knew about his ailment. He prescribed medicines responding to his present conditions from Ratnakar'report and gave medicines from his dispensary for immediate relief. Earlier, he expressed his inability to go to his house.

The next day his father was his usual self and wanted to go to the shop but Ratnakar's younger brother Kamaleshwar offered to open the shop in the morning and suggested he should come later if he felt better. His father did not want to take medicines as they, liquid or pills, tasted bitter, and put him in discomfort. The problem with him was that he couldn't gulp the pills down his throat, and so couldn't help chewing them. He was ultimately persuaded to take them as he liked and then he was free to go to the shop. He had to use rickshaw both ways for some days.

Ratnakar was sitting in his chair now across the table full of books crying out for dusting. Before he entered the room he knew what he had to do. So he had brought a towel with which to dust some books. He was surprised that he had all the text-books he needed for his elective subjects. They were all staring him from the table and the little shelf in the face in a comical way. What he missed, however, were notes explaining them which could help him answer questions in a balanced way. But he was confident he could do without them.

Lying on bed with a kerosene lantern on the chair beside the cot he began shuffling pages of an economics book. He found something relating to a question on the law of diminishing returns. He was engrossed in the study of examples when he suddenly came across a disconnect in his understanding. He tried to re-read the page. He again failed to connect one reason to another. He sat up and looked at the time in his alarm clock: it was 11.30 pm. Starting at 10 pm he could cover only two pages and that said it all. There was something wrong with his method of study if not with his intelligence. It was a shame in either case. When Shankar's Weekly needed to be read on a table how could he think of studying a text-book lying down on a cot? Something was decisively amiss with his life-style. He was casual about everything and perhaps not cut out for serious study. It was time; he looked at the clock for seventh time, for him to go to sleep for he was actually feeling sleepy. He still had time to decide.

CHAPTER THIRTY TWO

It was a clear sky with the Sun rising in all its glory in the winter that morning when he felt nature had plenty of beauty to distribute from one end of this planet to the other to make it a better place to live. A feeling of depression that overpowered him for the last few days began to disappear and he found himself transported to a green valley which was full of smell of different flowers. In the comforting warmth of the sunlight, sitting in the wooden chair in front of his house a question suddenly arose in his mind: Who was his first student (?) in the manner of "Who wrote the book 'My Experiments with Truth?' 'Which is the largest city in India'?" and so on. It was a patently absurd question to have occurred in Ratnakar's mind because factually he had yet to become a graduate which meant there was something wrong with his way of thinking, miles away from rationality. But the source of this question was what Chameli did or did not do. Yes it was she who made him her tutor on one occasion for a brief 2-week period or so.

"Ratnakar da, would you teach me this poem." Chameli caught me before he reached the library's window, with the text book open in her hand. Startled by the sudden waterfall of a question he looked back at her and at the piece she was pointing.

"But you'll have to give me time to read it." He said and extended his hand to take the book.

"Not here. Come to my place in the evening tomorrow. You'll have sufficient time to study it there and I'll have equal time to understand it. But," she paused," first clear it. Can you make it?" Ratnakar was surprised at this Chameli who put clearly what she wanted without any hesitation or shyness associated with a girl. It had certainly removed his image of her as a coy girl with limited words.

"I'm not sure about tomorrow right now. And you know why. But tomorrow in the college I'll confirm a date. That is, I'm coming though a date late." Ratnakar did feel awkward but he concealed it.

Since he had seen the piece he was expected to explain he collected materials on it, studied them sufficiently to talk about it for an hour or two in a reasonably good way. What he had grasped could last a couple of poems and this confidence made him feel he'd pass the test and impress her appropriately. Though he was by a certain standard a good speaker of English the same could not be said about his spoken Bengali as it left something to be desired. The question of Bengali came because whatever explanation he'd make in English had to be repeated in Bengali for her understanding. Learning would not be complete without it. And this was his weak point. Bengali must accompany his English utterances otherwise he'd end up impressing her without making her ready for answers in exams. Such teaching sessions which did not continue for many days did bring them closer to one another.

Ratnakar began to have dreams of her as a partner for life. An involuntary touch of her finger or adjusting of her saree's falling pallu, or the way she rose from the chair giving a glimpse of her rotundity, signaled new meanings for him. And he let his imagination float even if all this was quite away from the solid earth and enticingly hanging on its last point. Little girlish acts that are common.

And then . . . .

"Ratnakar da, will you go to Digha with me ?" Chameli asked him one day.

He looked into her black pools. Even though it was like her to say boldly things in the privacy of two he wanted her eyes to confirm it. He firmly clutched her arms and brought her a little closer to him to peer into her pools to find if it was not a mischief of some kind. She did not make any attempt to release herself from his catch.

"Yes, I will be tremendously happy to go with you. Tell me, when?" Ratnakar's dream was only some steps away from realization.

"I'll let you know soon." She said smilingly. "In the meanwhile I request you to find out how many buses are available in the morning between 7 and 8 for Digha. And . . ." She appeared to fumble for a right phrase.

"And return buses at sunset you mean . . ." Ratnakar tried to help her in finding the nearest phrase.

"Exactly that. Yes. I'm told it takes four hours to reach Digha from here. If so, we must get a 2 pm bus."

She thought aloud.

"But what about sunset scene, if you're really exploring Digha . . ." He said matt-of-factly. She merely looked at him. This was a question he should answer.

A little later she said, "Why did you touch my arms?"

This was a mood change or what; he was turning it in his mind.

"Do you resent it?" Ratnakar asked to find out the reason for this sudden change.

She did not say anything.

"Do you want me to say sorry?" Ratnakar was insistent. She did not reply.

They were talking near the road deserted at this hour near the college. She was waiting for her rickshaw at this spot far from the college gate to take her back home. She'd squeezed so much for him in that little wait. Actually he wanted her to stay a little more so that he could have some more from her but her rickshaw was already sighted speeding towards them.

"Wait here at 4 p m tomorrow." She said just before the rickshaw stopped before them.

Life is never monotonous. Even a cultivator who goes each morning to survey his field would affirm that life is anything but colorless as he experiences Monday is different from Sunday in more senses than one. So far as Ratnakar was concerned life did not follow expected turns.

Never. He was hoping for a durable relationship with Chameli as a friend. Not that he did not indulge in his personal dream of her as a romantic partner. It was therefore a crude shock to him when Chameli,instead of going to Digha with him, did go there after a fortnight of their talk, but without him, with someone else as her escort,guide or whatever. Of course,the dream-house that he built around her was shattered.

Ratnakar had, apart from Chameli-created mental shock, other problems too at that time and as they proved more pressing than his personal one he had to leave it at that. The imposing fact was that though the Party work had increased manifold the number of workers could not be increased proportionately. The Party had strict rules for enrolling members. One had to go through a long process to achieve it. At any time of the day and well into night the office was found humming with poster-writing, bundling and discussing slogans.

If Chameli's behavior was a shock he also had enough flexibility to absorb it, understand it, even sympathize with it. Later he realized it might be the result of some kind of his weakness or an inability to communicate with her in her metaphor. Perhaps he was not assertive enough to create confidence in her. Or a thousand other factors. He shouldn't be too fast in the matter of emotional entanglement and reach a conclusion that might turn out to be

based on far-from-reality object. Did he say or make her feel that he liked her in some especial way? A beautiful girl like her might have many friends. There's nothing unusual in this matter. The possibility of collecting a group of local friends for her Digha picnic could not be dismissed. The spice of her escort and guide bit might be incidental.

However much he might rationalize it he could not escape a pain in his heart somewhere.

All this receded in the background as he threw himself in the whirlwind of Party activities, off-college—hours. He looked around in the office. The tales of exploitation and grinding poverty forced his friends to think less of their personal problems and more of Party tasks.

CHAPTER THIRTY THREE

Whenever Ratnakar felt his mind overwhelmed by tug-of-war of competitive and contradictory thoughts he would turn to reading a Hindi novel, borrowed from a public library, courtesy Bindu Madhav, not just because Hindi was one of his subjects in BA course but because it could give him balm. Entangled in some intricacy of the novel he'd forget the surroundings. But this time around nothing seemed to attract him, nothing to arrest his attention. Exhausted he suddenly stopped reading the book and snapped it shut without even marking the page he was reading then.

It was a thought about Jayanta which had been disturbing him for quite some minutes and was not allowing him to proceed further. He got stuck for some minutes on a page and he closed it with some force. After becoming general secretary of students' union this would be the first occasion when Jayanta kept absenting

himself consecutively for six days of the week and there was no knowing whether he'd resume attending the college next week.

So far as Ratnakar was concerned everybody knew he had started preparing for the examination and was on his way out of the college soon. Despite this he who was alive to the responsibility entrusted to him bythe Party of looking after the organization of Students' Federation and the union couldn't neglect it. There was no day in the past when he did not accompany Jayanta to the college; he on rickshaw and Ratnakar on his cycle. Things had changed for both of them because of other duties' calls which could not be avoided.

It disturbed and pained him no end that he did not know the reason for his long absence. They were so close to each other that this communication gap looked a trifle intriguing, just unthinkable. If he was ill, the Party would have known it and since he was still a regular visitor to the Party office, the information could not have escaped his attention. There was something to it that intensified his curiosity as well as anxiety. He must go to Jayanta's house just then to satisfy himself about the cause of his inexplicable absence from college.

It took him 15 minutes to reach Jayanta's house by cycle and the door to his front

room being surprisingly open he did not have to knock it which was usually the practice. He was of course there but not in his chair, the usual place, but on the nearby cot, engrossed in reading some book.

"I was expecting you," he said seeing him enter the room and trying to get up from the bed. "Sit in the chair." He pointed to another chair.

"First tell me. Are you o.k.? Or really sick?" Ratnakar said bringing the chair close to him.

"Do I look like a sick man?" He said," But I'm not exactly o.k." He gazed at the window behind him thoughtfully as if he was talking to somebody else.

"You're talking in riddles. Why don't you come straight and tell me what's bothering you if you are really not sick. I believe you owe me that much as a . . . friend." Ratnakar wanted to get at the bottom of what was ailing him. He must find out the cause of his strange behavior.

"Well, Ratnakar, you're miles away from what's boiling in the Party. What you see at Kadampur Party office is not the whole face of it. There's more to it which is unhealthy and unsettling."

Jayanta said.

"What makes you think of these terrible things about the Party? And how is that you know about them and I don't?" Ratnakar was in a mode of interrogation.

"It is simple. These things are never discussed in any Party forum. There's no way of your knowingthe events that are thickly covered, you may say, sealed."

"If they are so thickly covered, then how is it that you penetrated the mystery? There must be some substance on which you're building this story or theory."Ratnakar made the right move now.

"Actually I didn't want to tell you so much." Jayanta said, "It was better if you did not know what I had undergone and felt. For a serious comrade like you it might be disappointing. To your question how I penetrated what you've called mystery my answer is that I was pushed into it by circumstances." He paused but only for a while and then spoke slowly, "I must tell you what makes me feel we are becoming puppets in the hands of a couple of puppeteers and ambitious leaders."Jayanta continued," I came across a senior Party member who asked me if I knew about a meeting of only a select few to be held at Barun da's house, and that it was to be addressed and presided over by state committee member Indranath Banerjee. I immediately contacted LCS Biren da who confessed his ignorance of any such meeting. The meeting-to-be was not held ultimately and Mishra da told me I was imagining things. Nothing was likely to happen without the local committee knowing it. But ", he said after a pause, "and this was the rub of the matter, I was called all the same by DCS Kanai da to district office where I was thrashed by Com. Indranath Banerjee for spreading rumor in his name and going beyond Party line.. He even threatened me with censure for anti-Party activities. I might even be stripped of Party membership. It was then that I said I have both—the Party Constitution and Programme—which gives me the right to go to control commission to defend myself against all charges. There were two other DC members in the room who felt the impact and implication of what I said. It was perhaps beyond their imagination that I could contradict and fight a tall leader like Indranath Banerjee in the DC office. They sweetened it by telling me this was advice and the meeting was over." Now Jayanta looked at me eyeball to eyeball and said," You got it, Ratnakar?"

"Yes I got it. A meeting of that nature, not permitted by the Party, was to be held. It could not take place because of you and that it was not a rumour. But I still don't see why you should keep away from the college." Ratnakar had a feeling that Jayanta was still hiding something.

"Then you haven't understood the implications of this tiff. The Party line is sabotaged by comrades who are sitting at the helm of affairs in the State. I heard there was something cooking in Calcutta when I was there last. I got confirmation of that from the attitude of Com. Indranath Banerjee. "

"How is that possible ? We have the same Party constitution and programme and we're in the Party because of them and not because of what Indranath Banerjee or for that matter anybody else said at one time or another concerning something or someone. "Ratnakar's uncertainty was growing even though he clung to the basic ideological position.

Jayanta laughed which dispelled the cloud somewhat." I'll go to college on Monday

next. In the meanwhile chew what is talked here. You've a long innings in the Party."

Ratnakar believed he got what he wanted. All he wished was he joined the college.

Though he did not rubbish the story Jayanta narrated he kept it aside for the time being.

It was 4 pm and his feet led him to the spot where he came on an earlier occasion in the hope of finding his love, the treasure. The students were still loitering before the college gate, waiting either for bus or their rickshaws. Since the college worked in two shifts, day students generally left the college by 4 pm which was the rule rather than the exception. Those who were still there at the gate were exceptions. Night students started coming after 5 pm. The college gate and its adjacent areas lined by tall trees with thick foliage on both sides of the road looked deserted between 4 and 5 pm. Ratnakar sat at the foot

of a tree and looked at the green field with his back on the passing road.

Suddenly he felt a touch of a soft hand on his shoulder. He turned back

only to see a surprise personified. It was Chameli trying to bend to sit beside him.

"What were you doing all alone here?" It wasn't so much an enquiry as a ground to begin some talk. She put the bag on one side and started locating something inside it.

"I don't think I can answer that question. I might be sitting here without any specific purpose".

"So you were not waiting for me?" She asked again.

"That was for a specific day. That's now past. History. Many events followed. Much

water flowed down the river Ganga. Why relate to them when you yourself erased

all of them."He was angry but in no mood to express it facially.

"Why don't you boys grow?" She said." You must grow up, Ratnakar da. I confess I

couldn't keep the appointment that day. But you shouldn't take it to heart that

seriously."

"You're saying it all as if that was all there was to it. One could observe there was more to it which you omitted I don't know why."

By this time she brought out her tiffin box from the bag. She tapped his shoulder

a couple of times and said,"Take this, I prepared it at home."Her eyes were imploring him.

What she was offering him was a "luchi" with its color gone yellow because of some

vegetable stuff in it. When he didn't make even the slightest move to take the "luchi", perhaps her first ever experiment at her kitchen-lab, or showed any interest in it she said slowly withdrawing her hand," Are you jealous ? I went to Digha with a mixed group of friends leaving you because I knew this might interfere with your studies for at least two days when everyday is crucial for you. Your studies were more valuable than Digha."

"But who wanted this explanation? You could go to Digha or any other place with your friends."Ratnakar said slipping a little on a side to make space between them.

"So you are not jealous?"She wanted an answer to this question.

"No."Ratnakar replied.

"Then what's wrong in taking this "luchi" and eating it? This is a food product. The only thing special about it is that I cooked it."

"Why are you getting sentimental about it when you don't attach any significance to others' sentiments?"Ratnakar expressed his feeling plainly.

"What do you mean by that? I respect the sentiments of others in the same way as I do mine, equally." She felt stung and flustered.

"What's your attitude to your failing of promise? I shouldn't have feelings? How should I have reacted to the appointment that never was." Ratnakar wasn't aware that he himself was a reservoir of sentiments.

"But I said I was sorry for that."

"No, you did not."

"I'm saying it now. I'm sorry for that."

Ratnakar snatched the "luchi" from her hand. Chameli felt rewarded but not sure whether she should be in tears or raptures of hilarity.

CHAPTER THIRTY FOUR

Nothing could be more blasphemous than to talk of Midnapur district in the context of communist movement in early 50s and 60s when the Party had just finished learning to crawl and not mention Neeta Chatterjee's name. Harinarayan Mishra never ceased to talk of her footwork in glowing terms. She worked hard to organize Kisan Sabha, Party's frontal organization, and the job took her to almost every village in her charge in the district, come rain or summer or cold. If Mishra da was not exaggerating, the inescapable conclusion was she was working at madness level at the call of the Party.

Ratnakar and some others were surprised to see the difference between her and Indranath Chatterjee, her husband, who instilled an unnamed fear and awe in them. The young lady moved, Florence Nightingale-like with a lighted candle of movement, from one village to another inspiring the villagers to join Kisan Sabha and the Party and strengthen them. Of course the development that followed was not the result of a single person's making but of collective functioning of veterans living at district headquarters leaving their families and all. She took individual interest in comrades of Kadampur including Ratnakar and was intimately popular among them because of her quality of making the comrade with whom she was talking feel at ease as the distinction between her station and his evaporated. In short Neeta di remained just Neeta di to one and all. Her frankness was reassuring.

But she was only an occasional bird at Kadampur as she mostly worked in villages assigned to her by the Party and lived in Tamluk and Calcutta. She never got on the wrong side of Kadampur Party's decisions and spoke only when asked. Harinarayan Mishra at that point of time enjoyed tremendous popularity at Kadampur. The respect between them therefore was mutual. This was revealed at political level too when differences started arising at district and State policies after the Party grew in shape and stature.

Ratnakar yesterday was at the Party office for sometime as Neeta di was expected to address a select gathering of students on their role in the changing society particularly rural scene. Though he did not participate in the meeting Neeta di met him and put a question disarmingly:"What are your plans after you pass out the examination?"

"I haven't thought about them. Let me first pass the exam."Ratnakar answered.

"The Party needs you. I'll be glad if you stay here. But if you go elsewhere we shall get in touch with you."

"I don't think I'm that important."

"You are."And she left.

Ratnakar went on repeating in his mind what Neeta di told him about his significance in the growing Party as he sipped his familiar cup of tea in the bistro __ the one near the college. He kept coming to the college more to keep his sanity than for any official discharge of the function of vice-president which though he still was."What are your plans after you pass out the examination?" was the question posed by Neeta di. No plans. It was darkness that haunted him.

"Ratnakar da, how is that you're sitting alone in this corner? Whatever happened to your friend?"

It was the voice of Swapna Jana. He turned to say something, and then thought the better of it as she continued "Am I intruding upon your thoughts?"

"On the contrary, you are welcome and this answers both your questions." Ratnakar replied with a smile.

"How smart! You've neatly put the burden on others. On me. I know I've interfered with your thought process. Now tell me what were you really thinking. That is, if you take me to be your friend." Words flowed from her as she sat on the chair facing him across the table.

"Will you believe it if I tell you I was thinking why you could not be seen in Neeta di's meeting?" Ratnakar leaned forward with his elbows on the table to be closer to her face to emphasize his idea.

"And who, by the way is Neeta di? And why should I attend her meeting?"

"My goodness. It appears nobody in my absence is interested in talking about Party's identity. Neeta di is a leader of the CPI.She's an ideal of a leader. She could have been glad to see you there. You missed a chance, I'd say."He felt his words were not going well with her so he stopped.

"Ratnakar da, let me make it clear to you. I'm ready to do anything you ask me to in the college. I've got that liberty. But beyond the walls of this college I have to think twice before I act. I hope you would appreciate it. " She said seriously but in a low tone with a tinge of apology.

"But why should you follow me in the college?"Ratnakar put a basic question.

"Because I like . . . ." She trailed. Ratnakar looked at her straight as if prompting her to finish.

"Because I like you." She made a great statement in a simple sentence. "I was hoping you would say it—you would be the first to declare your feeling—but you allowed the chance to lapse. You did not."She rose up to go.

"Hey, stop. You can't beat me that way. What do you think I came here for today." Ratnakar's voice was too loud to be missed by some others sitting at far-end tables. At this Swapna sat down.

"How do I know for what purpose you came here today? I'm not a mind-reader." She calmed down."I cannot be clearer than what I said. You stopped me to say something. Now say what."

"I came here to find my lost thread. And the lost thread is you. You are my rose. You are my dream."He couldn't help being a bit romantic and sentimental uttering these words which never grow old or stale.

She immediately put both her hands on the table and said, "You touch my hands and repeat slowly what you just said."

He put his hands on her hands saying "I love you"

"That will do. Now can you come to Gole Bazar and meet me at the new restaurant Noorjehan at 7 p.m. today?"

Things were racing too fast for him and he was . . .

"Don't worry about the bill. I'll pay it." She was smiling in a mischievous way.

"Are you going to demolish your earlier statement that you are not a mind-reader? It appears you can do something more. Don't forget I'm a male partner." And he laughed. "We shall discuss that when we meet again. I shall wait for you near the restaurant at 7p.m." And she stood up to meet her other friends who started coming in there.

He felt after her departure that he had a new experience that he never encountered earlier in life. The waves in his heart were getting tumultuous. And why shouldn't they? He never knew what it was to be wanted by a girl. His mind was racing with all kinds of thoughts at once. Chameli,for one,would not like to be compared with any other girl damned as she was with her own beauty. She herself never took relations seriously as she had more suitors than she could keep count of. In no case was she his cup of tea, he reminded himself. This perhaps he did for the nth time.

Swapna, an inch taller than Ratnakar, had the power to create emotions in him that might become uncontrollable. Suddenly the thought struck him: Swapna had the makings of a Neeta Chatterjee. But he dismissed this thought as soon as it came. Swapna was unlike anybody on this planet for him because she was his Swapna.

Ratnakar could not deceive himself as he knew his weak spots, social and academic. When others succeeded in memorizing a passage or a quotation after 3 or four attempts he would take at least 10 shots to do the same thing and even at the end of these exercises he couldn't be sure if he was correct. And so far as social relations were concerned he knew none beyond the circle of the Party. If any relatives came to his house on a social call he just did not know how to deal with the situation, what to talk to them. Yes, frankly he was at a loss to find a proper attitude to take and words to speak.

Will he succeed in getting Swapna's love? She said she liked him. She might change her idea about him if she came more close to him. The thought was disturbing.

He did not remember of making any serious effort to get closer to her except maybe mental at some fleeting moment. And here she proposed this meeting—at Noorjahan.He was afraid that something might happen just before the event and he might fail in reaching the place on time. The consequence was well understood. Just then he heard the ear-splitting sound of lightning not very far away in the sky. Nothing could be more ominous than this warning as if the Nature had synchronized with his deep-seated fear. But it was just 4 p.m. He still had some hours. He must reach Noorjahan restaurant at 6.30 P.M., come rain or hail—storm or cloudburst.

Surprisingly and to his great relief the rain stopped and the sky became clear at 6 p.m.with no trace of even a lingering cloud as a couple of twinkling stars assured every sky-gazer. Within 10 minutes of his reaching the spot Ratnakar saw Swapna alighting from a rickshaw. He rushed to her and stood the cycle on the stand in front of the restaurant while she gave instructions to the rickshaw driver to which he nodded in agreement.

It was unusual for a new restaurant of this fashion to have so few customers at this hour though it had got great notice and fulsome praise from those who enjoyed the delicacies of Noorjahan. They had a table to themselves.

The working boy promptly put the menu on the table and went back perhaps to serve other customers.

"What would you like to have?"Swapna asked him looking at the menu.

"I'm not good at choosing items in a restaurant of this size. I'll go with you."

"There's chicken cutlet, Moglai paratha and . . ." She looked sharply at him and said, "I didn't see you take any non-vegetarian preparation at the college. Are you a veg by any chance?"

"Yes, I am. But I'll still go with you. I see no reason why you are being so considerate of me." He retorted.

"Only for once. You may take dosa. And here's for you dhakai paratha—an ancient cuisine." She signaled the bearer to come and ordered a dosa for him and a moglai paratha for herself.

"I hope you don't feel uncomfortable sitting with me in this public place. You know I'm not quite an unknown quantity in some parts of the town. It's a small town." Ratnakar said as he failed to find any better topic to talk.

"I know people are familiar with your face. The bearer who looked at you was smiling in recognition."

"And yet you brought me to this place where I can't kiss you or even hold your hand."

"You've to grow for that. Learn to wait . . ."She said.

"The boy was smiling because he thought you're not my class and . . . ." Before he completed his statement the bearer came and the table was served.

CHAPTER THIRTY FIVE

When Ratnakar was driving his cycle towards Party office after a royal gap of time busy as he was with studies he saw an arresting though not unfamiliar site of a riot of flowers—marigold, jasmine, red rose and mixed petals—spread over a sizable patch of the road suggesting there was a big festival on the previous night. One could guess it was a ceremonial marriage. The stench of stale food which littered on both the sides of the road could not overpower the residual smell of flowers. He felt amused at the flowers' lovers who must have spent quite a fortune on them. But you don't ask the choice of this kind of display in a working class area as even heart had a day off __ if you insist__ from mind. Whatever it was, it had set Ratnakar's mood right.

It was 10 A. M. The Party office was certainly crowded unusually for this morning hour. But what he heard there in the hushed silence from his close friends surprised him and dampened his spirit. The previous night there was a meeting of local committee members,each elected from a different branch of Kadampur Party, where Harinarayan Mishra,MLA, the senior most comrade, was criticized by a majority. Reduced to figures the picture stood :8 criticized,2 remained silent,2 supported his acts. Ratnakar was not given any details about the meeting nor did he seek them.

But Ratnakar was not happy even with this small discordant happening. Naveen Mitra, who was usually writing and artistically decorating posters with his brush, could not be found in this crowd. So there was a good possibility that he was at home, and away from this office he might be more forthcoming on yesterday's episode.

"What happened now in the students 'front?" Naveen Mitra asked him when he entered his room.

"Nothing of significance to give anxious moments. But . . . ."

"Are you coming from Office right now or from your house?"Naveen Mitra asked him.

"From Party office . . . You can guess why I came to you." Ratnakar said, "As the office was overcrowded LCMs kept mum about yesterday's meeting. But they conveyed vaguely that the Party is up against a big problem without being specific about it."

"At the moment the Party has no problem. But it's going to have one very soon."Naveen Mitra continued, "You're grown enough to make a difference between an ideology and its application. It's one thing to call yourself a communist and another to practice it in your life. Mishra da started developing some harmful tendencies after he had become MLA. Salute by Government officers and being "sirred" by one and all men of substance have gone into his head."

"Are you jealous of it?"Ratnakar's question was frank but it did not disturb Mitra da who said," Since you have brought it to the personal level you must follow this reasoning why it's not jealousy. He's a senior leader here and he'll always have this place. But what answer you have if our political antagonists say that it's not the Party that won the election but Mishra da did with the force of his personality, and because they love him for his jumping into any fray in favor of the people. He's developing this cult. He's crediting all the work done for public good by the Party to his personal account. Is it, or is it not a fact that the Party did most organizationally facing hurdles and dangers day and night before and after the election ? Yesterday's meeting attempted to check him."

"Where did you put a brake on him?" Ratnakar once again asked.

"It was the same old story. He's the highest collector for the Party no doubt. Now more than ever. He fulfills the personal quota fixed for him. But he collects more and that's the rub of the matter. It's not that he keeps the money for personal use. He gives money to sick comrades, needy comrades out of the undisclosed purse. He likes to feel that he's doing personal favor to them. That's one reason. A senior comrade, Kanti da, was weeping the other day for being shouted down before so many comrades for forgetting to collect a subscriber's due. This couldn't be supported by any means. Most branch comrades don't see any deviations in him from party principles now but they will after sometime." Naveen Mitra stopped and laughed."You got all you wanted to know. Now go and organize students."

"But Naveen da, we've heard such criticisms even earlier. My point is that if he works harder than any of us he certainly deserves a greater part of the cake. Calling in the argument of deviations is sounding a bit trite." Ratnakar felt.

"You still have the old measurement of assessing him. It is traditional, and sentimental. You forget that none of us joined the Party looking at anybody's face. It is ideology that finally attracted us. We judge things on the basis of ideology. We sacrificed something for it. We still go on doing it. "Naveen Mitra said.

It was noon and he was in his study after a hurried bath. He wore white pajama and shirt, both newly washed and was waiting for his lunch. But despite all the outer freshness he was still far from feeling happy or enthusiastic about the flow of life. His session with Naveen Mitra did not remove the darkening clouds. His idols, one after another, were breaking and melting under the heat of realism's gaze. Clearly he himself was responsible for starting on a negative vibe as no other Partyman thought like he did. What was happening was the way of the world, to them. Just then someone whispered in his ear: Now you've only one week to prepare for final BA examination. Rudely awoken from his reverie he rushed to his lunch place.

Nobody came to see him throughout this period—before and during the examination. Suddenly the whole world turned sympathetic to him. Examination came and went leaving him face to face with a vacuum. There was nothing, absolutely nothing, for him to do now. He clung to the hope that he would succeed in this attempt but he ruled out further opportunity to go in for higher study. The only option that lay before him was to seek a job. Where?

Kadampur being a railway town people depended on it for a living as workers or small shop-keepers. They could not think beyond them. Railway Service Commission for educated young men and apprenticeship for lesser boys was the way out for a try. But they came once in a year. No other candidate was more fit to be turned out from the gate than Ratnakar in the event of his application. That left him a teacher's job. And why was he so desperate for a job even before the results were out. The answer lay in the reality that even to love someone needed money. And he was truly in love with Swapna. Even though he was not a poet he composed a couple of poems for Swapna which he sang in privacy forgetting he ridiculed some of his friends for doing precisely that just some time ago. She might like the poems and feel happy about them but they could not replace money which alone could buy transport, hotel bills and little gifts. What was his status in this department?

Ratnakar passed the BA Exam with better marks than most students of the college which was saying a great deal about his proficiency. While this satisfied his friends and family, this also silenced the prophets of his doom. As if he cared.

His main concern was to get a job but the ordinary route to it was multi-stepped and circular. Waiting for an advertisement like "Wanted a teacher in . . . ." was time-consuming and disheartening. Since he was the seeker of the job he decided he must take the first step of moving to schools and say to the managing committees that he needed a job. He started on this unconventional mission and crossed the town's boundaries with a load of "No vacancy". He was already 15 miles away from Kadampur and well into a forest area with a cycle which was equally exhausted. It's not what he came looking for when he started this Columbus mission. He began his journey back to Kadampur with the darkness covering the area slowly at the sunset and by the time he reached his house it was already night.

Ratnakar lived in two worlds _ the world of illusion and the world of reality. In his sleep that night in his study he experienced a relief that came after washing of brain and body. He was enjoying the feeling of sinking slowly and yet more slowly down. Suddenly he felt he was left in a tunnel and as it happened there was no light at the end of it.

Unbeknown to himself he put his hand inside his pocket and felt the existence of a scrap of paper. It electrified his mind and body to remind him that some two days ago Swapna gave him a paper which he kept in his trousers' pocket and forgot about it. Was it the same paper? She scribbled praise or criticism about his poems which he read many times over in his private moments to find any hidden meaning.

When he put on the lantern he found it was Swapna's scribbled slip with a date and time for meeting. She wanted him to accompany her from college to some place in the Southside. The slip was staring him in the face. How could he forget about this slip all the past hours? Thankfully, the date was to come the next day but it shook him all the same.

Since it was a different kind of assignment he came by rickshaw to the college instead of on his ubiquitous cycle.

"Thank you for coming here." Swapna blossomed." I thought after becoming a graduate, you lost interest in the college." It was meant to be jibe.

"What made you think so? Being a graduate has nothing to do with coming to college."

"But your friends said they did not know about your whereabouts to my specific questions concerning you. So I've to conclude . . . ." She threw up her hands imitating some mannerism.

"Well, I was actually out searching some job most of the time . . ."

"But why are you in a hurry for a job . . . so early? "She laughed.

It was this innocence that won Ratnakar over many times. He could not tell her that even to love her cost money which, to put it frankly, was in short supply for him. A passing rickshaw-driver was stopped by her and instructions were given to him. When he dropped them at the destination it was already dark and the direction she took had for some reason no light though there were electric poles. She stopped in front of the gate of a bungalow. Ratnakar waited for a "Thank you ".

Instead she said,"We shall have coffee together. I'll prepare it myself. You deserve it for the act." Ratnakar was not sure whether it was sarcasm or a sincere expression of thankfulness.

"Keep the coffee for some other time. I want this."

"What . . ."She turned her face towards him. And he kissed her in the mouth putting all the emotion in the stopped time _ a soulful kiss that lasted eternity.

"Stupid . . . . Come in I'll make coffee. But this wasn't fair."

He was confused: She did not protest when she was being kissed.

"How would your parents react when they see me with you at this hour? Ratnakar hesitated.

"Now get in, I say." Her voice got stentorian, though subdued."We can discuss these things even inside. It's cold outside."

He followed her instructions. There was no one inside that little bungalow. She put on all the lights. When she was warming up coffee he had a peek at the sky: The stars were glinting in divine jealousy of the moon which exuded its nonchalance.

When he had sipped half the cup of coffee he asked her: "When are your parents expected to be back?"

"It is an accident that this bungalow is deserted till 4 PM next day. And it so happens I've nowhere else to go." There was a sly smile on her lips but only for a moment.

This was her way of putting the card on the table. After a pause he said,"Do you believe I'd leave you in this situation and seek safe shelter elsewhere?"

She did not respond.

"Say something."

"No comment." She replied.

"Got anything for night's dinner?"

"Enough food. Items need only heating up." She started to move. He followed her.

"Is this your bedroom?"

"Yes."

"I take rest here while you . . ." And he went straight for the bed and sat on it. She came back and sat beside him.

"I love you. I love you."Ratnakar repeated as he felt loving vibes in the room.

'I heard it."

Ratnakar drew her close and embraced her, the sensitive peaks of her breasts pressing softly into his chest. She tried to wriggle out of this position saying "This isn't proper "but her resistance became weaker by seconds while he straightened himself on the bed pulling her over him on the bed pulling her over him by one hand, and she was slowly slipping into the quilt and over him.

Ratnakar found a reason for living in the world of struggle while Swapna discovered herself in Ratnakar.